WOUNDED

WARRIORS

MATRIX FILIA & CLAUDETTE WALKER

Abacus Books, Inc.
P.O. Box 55302
St. Petersburg, Florida 33732-5302, U.S.A.
www.abacusbooks.com

Library of Congress Cataloging in Publication Data
Filia, Matrix & Walker, Claudette
WOUNDED WARRIORS
I. Title

EAN# 978-0-9716292-0-2

Printed in the United States of America
Set in Times New Roman

Dedicated to the soldiers of war

and their families.

From The Authors

For many years, we have all been touched by soldiers' lives upon returning home from war. Too often, we have seen that the excitement of coming home leaves them little time to decompress. This book has been inspired by soldiers' stories. However, those stories are here only to emphasize the realities of war and the needs of those returning. Many require a way to unwind. We realize that a person who lives through combat is forever changed. There is no magic potion to erase the memories of war's reality.

However, we pondered a new method for bringing members of the military out of war zones and back home. We are proposing a way for them to take a little time to return to civilian life without great expectations placed upon them. This method can be applied by the soldiers themselves, their mates, friends, families or other loved ones who knew them before the war.

We hope this novella inspires the reader to look outside the box for methods to comfort newly returning soldiers and those soldiers who have been home for years. Giving them a little decompression map may be one way to do so. Our warriors have certainly earned our understanding and support. Please enjoy our inspirational story.

We have provided a guide and a place for your own decompression map and a journal for soldiers' memories in the back of this book. We hope soldiers on their own journeys will make notes in the journal for themselves. We suggest each keep it close for the future, as a way to preserve memories of the time he or she spent decompressing. Each one's map and journal will be a different journey in life.

Welcome home…

WAR

Matrix Filia & Claudette Walker

Sergeant Josh Smith, 100328197. The deployment clock started ticking when he reported for duty at Dover. In one year and seventy-one hours, he would be out of a hellhole and back on home soil. Josh stood at Dover Air Force base next to a '67 convertible in desperate need of repair while saying goodbye to his wife, the beautiful redheaded Lucy. He had been deployed for one hour and was about to get on a military transport plane. Josh was leaving for Afghanistan, a desert paradise – at least that is what the brochure said. It is a moment in time that has happened all over the world. This could be any soldier's story…

Dover Air Force Base, May 5:

Disharmonious sounds seemed to blend into a perfect thunderous roar. It was clear which groups of passing soldiers were coming back and which were leaving for overseas. Anyone who looked could see the fear and excitement of new recruits going off to their first deployment and the beaten, exhausted, yet wiser look of those just returning.

The planes were poised in perfect harmony to take their place on the runway. The transports were waiting to carry their human cargo to faraway destinations. In front of them were families and soldiers trying to act like it was business as usual. But they all knew that with war, nothing is usual.

Lucy wrapped hers arms tightly around Josh "Love you. A year is too long."

"I love you too, Luce. But it'll go by quickly, I hope. Just find us a house and get out of that apartment."

She laughed and gave Josh an almost childish look. "What, you don't like our 300 square feet and the view of the ugly, naked guy?"

Aircraft engines roared as a plane took off above them and Josh screamed his response. "Very funny! I've grown to like him. That's beginning to scare me. Still, I'm not thrilled about leaving you in LA. I know we can't afford much, but try to find a small town."

After the plane passed overhead, Josh lowered his voice.

"You pick – anywhere you want in California. The price of real estate there makes it almost impossible to rent, let alone buy anything bigger than a shoebox. Find us something out of the city – even somewhere in the desert would be fine with me. One day, we'll live near the ocean,

I promise! It's just that there's no way we can afford it now."

Lucy nodded and started giggling. "Okay, so Malibu it is! I think if I look hard enough, we could afford to rent closet space in a billion-dollar mansion. Then again, maybe not."

Their idle conversation could not fill the void caused by Josh's imminent departure, but somehow it helped. "Very funny, Lucy. I just wish I had more time to look for a place with you before I deployed."

"Me too, but I'll find us a new house fast. I'll stay with my parents 'til I get us out of LA. Don't worry about me hon. I'll be careful, I promise. Just be safe and get home to me. I love you!"

"I love you too. I'll be back. I know how independent you are; that's something that attracted me to you in the beginning, and it's still one of the things I love about you."

"Thank you; remember that while you are there. Tell your buddies you have a self-sufficient, stubborn, redheaded woman at home. Tell 'em if anything happens to you, I'll come to your camp and there'll be hell to pay."

Josh let out a guttural laugh. "I'm sure no one wants to be on the receiving end of your wrath.

It could come in handy with the enemy, though. Maybe I can just tell them that instead of shooting at 'em. Maybe it would work – you never know."

Lucy looked at Josh seriously and told him, "LA is too dangerous anymore, either with or without you! I'll get us a place somewhere. It may not be our dream house, but I'll find something."

"You're right, it was one thing during college, but now… I knew I needed to get out even before we got married. I love you more than you know. I'll make it back and won't worry about you; at least, not much."

Josh's trademark wink gave Lucy a kind of peace. "I know you'll be safe with your parents for now." Josh tapped the hood of the old convertible. "I sorta wondered if Old Lucy would make it here in one piece. It's a long way from California to Delaware. As good as this car did getting here, I know she'll get you home. I'll get her restored when I get back – she sure has earned it, and I've wanted to do that for a long time."

Josh gave Lucy's arm a squeeze. "But getting married to the girl of my dreams was more important! I'll Skype when I can. That's one advantage to being assigned to FAC. Probably the only one, if my guess is right. I still can't believe they sent me to school to learn aircraft targeting systems for this job, just 'cause I got my private pilot's license when I was fifteen! This is supposed to be an assignment for a military pilot, but I guess the rules get pretty badly bent in wartime." The sound of voices calling Josh's platoon stopped their light-hearted banter.

"I just want you to be careful, whatever they have you doing."

They saw the soldiers in Josh's platoon beginning to line up, preparing to march toward a plane. They embraced and each delivered one long last kiss. "I have to go. I love you."

Lucy gave Josh big smile, trying to hide her tears. "I love you too." He ran to catch up with the others, looking back only once to give her a smile. Saying goodbye is never easy, especially if you know it could be the last time.

Seventy-two hours later, Josh was in the hot mess of Gangikhel, Afghanistan, riding in a military convoy moving through a decrepit war zone. As an FAC, forward air controller, Josh was sitting at the communications and fire controls of a satellite-equipped Humvee. That was where he would be day after day for the next year.

His buddy Martini was driving, as he had always done. Martini was a hell of a smooth driver, which was not easy in that terrain. After what seemed like twenty lifetimes of bouncing around in Humvees, they were finally on their last run together before Josh prepared to leave Afghanistan in thirty days. They were in a convoy headed back to camp, the mission almost complete.

Josh heard and felt the silence. His big brother Dave told him to watch out for that stillness before Josh left home for this godforsaken place. He also told Josh that when things get too quiet in war, something really bad was about to happen. Dave made it home alive from Iraq several years ago and understood all too well what it was like.

"Man, Martini, everything is wiped out here. There's nothing left, nothing's moving or making any noise – it's too quiet." They both looked around at the vacant open area, knowing that looks can be deceiving.

"Yeah, it's too still."

"Martini, this is an eerie silence… I'm going to run a scan again."

Martini was peering at the horizon to the east of the Humvee. "Zoom to the east."

Josh calls out, "Nothing…Shit! They're to the north! Incoming!" The lead vehicle in the convoy suddenly was taking mortar fire, but the rounds missed their mark. Josh called in a strike with a point and click of his joysticks that controlled a red box on the computer screen. The box read: STRIKE 32 35 54 92N 69 19 0362E LIVE NO PHOSPHOROUS.

Live fire from allies was then coming over the satellite communications Humvee and the rest of the convoy. It took out the threat to the north that had just begun to fire on the trucks. A green square showed on the screen, along with the words HOLD FIRE, then in a moment, CLEAR.

"Damn! All clear, Martini." Sweat poured down the inside of Josh's helmet, stinging his eyes. Martini shook his head. "I knew it was too quiet! That was close! Nice shootin', Smith. Let's get back to base and get you home. I don't want a certain redhead coming after me." Both men started to laugh, relieving their tension a little. "Trust me, you don't want to be on Lucy's bad side." The convoy continued its return to camp. "Martini, that was too damn close! It's like they knew this was my last ride. Well, to hell with them and their antique Soviet weapons! We made it!"

"Good call, Josh. Live, no foss. That's a brave one! They missed the convoy and you didn't hit us either! Let's get in front and spot, until we get this convoy back. These guys would be really pissed off if we get 'em killed just returning to camp. I bet they're shitting their pants at the live fire coming over their heads!" Josh's eyes lit up with a huge grin and he slapped the dash with his hand. "For sure! Man, I hated that call, but by the time they would've shown us the lights, we'd all have been dead!"

A voice came over the radio from another convoy Humvee to the communications vehicle. It was Mark Applehead. "Great shot guys – not a dry pair of pants in this tin can! Good going!"

Josh laughed, "Sorry, no time for foreplay, Applehead. By the time I would've seen the lights, we'd all been road kill. Live fire with no warning was our only chance!" Josh can hear cheering in the background over the radio.

"Man, I know Josh, I know. I'm just glad it was you making that call. A few degrees off and we'd be toast."

"You know, Applehead, that's why I get the big bucks! You can pay me back with your peaches tonight!"

The sergeant's laughter bellowed above the noise the soldiers were making in the background. "No way, Smith! You're gonna be eating real food in no time! Tonight, that short-timer's stick is yours – as soon as we get back to camp. Shit man, I'm really going to miss those calls."

"Hey Applehead, it's Martini. I feel the same!"

Applehead, as Martini's sergeant, tried to reassure his soldier. "Yeah, but at least we're getting Sims on loan from the British 'til we get a replacement – they don't come any better! You know what I mean, Smith."

Josh smiled reflexively, even though Applehead could not see it, as he replied, "We all know it's shit, luck, and ignorance out here! We heard the silence; that's what started us scanning! It helps that they got the video game generation for this war!" Josh made joystick moves with his hands like he was playing a game. "Yeah, and momma said those video games would be the death of me!"

The convoy made it safely back to camp one more time. Each soldier high-fived Josh, as they got out of the vehicles. Josh's replacement, Sims, was waiting and handed him his coveted short-timer's stick. It had thirty circles carved around its shaft, one for each day remaining. He had been waiting for this! Sims was from Manchester, England and sharp as a tack. "Here you are Josh! I'll take it from here.

Congratulations on that last strike. What a way to go out..."

Applehead interrupted, "Yeah, we'll carry the load from here. Thirty days and you're out of these damn mountains and home free."

Martini jumped in with his thick Bronx accent, "At least Sims is a partner who's classier than the last one! Speaking of classy, I think you should leave Lucy's picture as a pin-up for us. You're one lucky son of a bitch; you got a wife with beauty and brains!"

Applehead had been teasing Josh nonstop about Lucy since he saw a picture of her in a bikini. "Come on, Smith! Just one pic for those you're leaving behind."

Josh reached in his wallet and pulled out few pictures. "In your dreams, guys! No way I'm leaving a swimsuit pic – but maybe she wouldn't mind being your pin-up, if you guys get me out of here alive. I'll ask her. Keep your fingers crossed!"

Martini gave him a bear hug. "Josh, you're on easy street! You'll be baking in the California sun and catching waves in no time."

Thoughts of returning to Lucy and lying on the beach swam through Josh's mind. Those dreams were much closer to reality for him. "Martini, I can feel the waves now."

Applehead said with a chuckle, "Nope, that's wet pants from the last call," Everybody started laughing and making funny kissing faces to Josh.

Then Martini stood up and rehashed what happened in the truck as it all went down. "You saw it, Applehead – that was spot on! The first rounds missed and Josh got them before they could get off any more!"

Applehead shook his head yes while walking over to Josh and patting him on the back. "I saw it Martini, Live, no foss! Too much! We'll miss you, Smith."

As the soldiers settled in their tents for the night, Josh headed to the communications area to Skype Lucy with the news. Her image came up on the computer, and he proudly displayed his short-timer's walking stick. "Baby, I got it! Can you see it?"

She leaned in closely to the camera. "Yes, I see it. Why do I still hear bombs?"

"Hon, this is a war zone. This short-timer's stick means I don't have to go out on patrols, especially night patrols, and I won't guard the camp perimeter or other routine hazardous duty.

That's 'cause I only have 30 days left. But if the shit hits, I'm still in the fight!"

She smiled but tried to keep from jumping when the bombs went off in the background. "That's great! Congrats, baby! Sorry, the noise just caught me off guard. I'm thrilled and counting the days! I just want you home. I miss you so much!"

Seeing her porcelain skin and the sleepy look on her face made him eager to get back. Even on a computer screen, she was beautiful. "I'll be home soon. Any chance you're going to show me more of the new house?"

She repositioned the camera to make sure that not much was in view. "Nope, you will just have to get here and see for yourself. You'll love the place. You can see the kitchen, I think."

Josh leaned into the screen but could only make out what looked like a fridge, maybe. "That's not the room I want you in!"

"Well then, hurry on back, soldier!"

"By the way Lucy, the guys want me to leave a picture of you for them as a pin-up. I told them no bathing suit."

The corners of Lucy's mouth made a half smirk. "You're in a war zone with a bunch of nuts! But sure, I can give that much to the war effort. Although I think I could find some prettier women on Venice Beach."

"I don't think so! My wife has already been voted the most beautiful woman in the world – by me! Okay, I guess my reluctance to have my gorgeous wife leered at by a bunch of goofballs is not so smart, after all. Why shouldn't they enjoy a picture – I'll have the real thing! Martini and the guys can have one if they get me out alive."

Lucy's face looked faintly serious. "What do you mean if? Josh Smith, you are coming home! Promise them a bathing suit shot if you need to. Just tell them to guard that camp!"

"Like I told you Luce, I'll be there soon. You know, promising that photo could just do it. Bribery does work around here!"

The sun was coming up in California; Josh could see the light faintly glowing behind Lucy's head. "I'm waiting! Just tell them they can have any damn picture they want once they get you out of there!"

"I'm coming, but it's like Dave said, I'm going to need some time to decompress before I'll be fit company. How is my brother?"

"I understand baby, I see it every day at the VA. Your brother, Linda, and the kids are fine.

They're as excited as me to get you home. I've been thinking about your need to decompress. Your brother told us both that you'll need some time for that after the war. He remembers how hard it was for him after Iraq. Do you still like maps after all this?"

With a perplexed but intrigued look, he answered her. "You know I do, baby! Yeah, even after this place, I still love maps. I want us to travel like we planned – take a map and just drive. That'll be as soon as we can get Old Lucy restored. I don't know if that car has another long road trip left in her without some work."

"Well, at least she's still running." Sitting in the driveway was a fully restored Lucy. His wife and family were keeping the restoration a closely held secret until Josh got back to the States. "Hey, I have an idea. Go with me on this."

"I'll go anywhere with you!"

Lucy grinned and said, "Remember, Dave said if anyone meets you at Dover Air Force Base, it'll take a lot longer to get you home. You know, security screening and the like. But if no one is meeting you there, they'll do a quick debriefing and you'll be on the next commercial flight to LAX fast! Besides, I'd hate to break down on the way to get you."

Josh looked momentarily confused, wondering what she had planned. He said, "Yes, I do know, and I'd hate to be on my way to Dover wondering if Old Lucy was going to strand you. So, we'll meet me at LAX?"

"Baby, you know how much I love you. I want nothing more than to meet your plane. Instead, I'm sending Dave to bring you home to me. I've been working on a little map for you guys to follow. It'll be fun."

Josh frowned briefly, as he thought about having to wait even longer to see his bride. After only a moment, his mood brightened again at the thought of an adventure with his brother. Containing his excitement had never been easy for Josh, and since practically everyone was sleeping, he just grinned from ear to ear. "That's my Lucy – always in for a little fun! And Dave picking me up, bringing me to you is brilliant! God, I miss him, too!"

The sounds of bombs exploding were getting louder in the background. "Lucy, incoming is getting closer. We're gonna get disconnected soon. I'll try to call again."

Her face saddened a bit. "I hear them. Stay safe. Are you in for giving my map a try?"

Josh nodded. "Anything to get back to my baby! I'm going to lose this connection." The last image he saw was Lucy blowing a kiss into the camera before the connection failed. Bombs were exploding everywhere and the camp was shaking. Josh and a few others were vibrating with the blast.

Lucy's last words before they were disconnected were running through his head. "I'll be waiting for you! I love... and then everything went dark. It was a hell of a way to end a conversation, because Josh knew Lucy would be wondering if he was okay, or if that loss of connection meant that something terrible had happened. He also knew he could do nothing about it – comm was down. She would just have to worry until the next time he could contact her. He hoped it would be soon.

Josh headed off to his rack, trying to survive the next month so he could be with her again. He also needed to get a little shut-eye before the night patrol headed out. Even though Josh was not going this time, he wanted to see his buddies off.

Late that night, outside the tents of Camp Barrique, the patrols were preparing to leave. Martini and Sims, his new co-pilot, were about to get into the Humvee.

Josh called out, "Martini, keep low out there. Sims has your back. See you in the morning."

Sims turned and gave Josh a smile saying, "Thanks for the vote of confidence, Josh. I'll take care of Martini."

"Thanks, Sims – you know Martini's my buddy, so I'm gonna hold you to that! Besides, you've done dozens of these runs. Stay safe!"

Martini, never forgetting the important things, swiveled in his seat and yelled over the rumbling engine, "Did you tell Lucy we want her to be our pin-up?"

Sims quickly chimed in, "Speak for yourself!"

"Okay, Sims, but the guys want her picture!"

As Sims made a face, Josh laughed at Martini – always the class clown, but he had his priorities. "She said you're all nuts! If you get me out of here alive, you can have a bathing suit shot, but not until you get me out of this war zone. I'm not looking at my wife's picture on your wall!"

Martini laughed and smirked as he gave a half wave goodbye. "Cool, we'll see you in the sunshine!" Then he closed the door and signaled Sims that it was time to get rolling.

Sims nodded to Josh as she clambered into the Humvee. "Don't worry Josh; I have his back. Later!"

Josh held his stick up and waved back as they pulled away, calling out, "See ya!"

He went into the tent to watch the convoy's movements on a computer. The bombs were getting closer and closer to it, when suddenly a loud alert sound came across the screen. Coordinates were lighting up and Josh saw that Sims was beginning to fix on a target. His blood pressure was soaring and it felt like his heart was beating out of his chest. He watched, praying she would lock on the target.

A direct hit on the communications vehicle filled one of the screens. Josh could see the explosions off in the distance through the open doorway of the tent. In disbelief, his attention returned to the computer screen as he stared, devastated and guilt-ridden.

He felt vomit rising in his throat. "Come on! Oh, Martini! Sims! Fuck! Fuck!"

Josh grabbed a computer headset and frantically tried to call Martini and Sims on the radio.

"Martini, come in! Martini, answer me! Sims, come in! Come on, answer me! Fuck!"

There was no response from the vehicle. Josh began to hit things with his stick and then ran outside the tent. The entire camp was carrying on with business as usual – no one else yet realized that the explosion was the convoy taking fire. If the worst was true, soldiers would be quieter and more solemn for a while, but their work could not pause for the deaths of allies. The war went on.

Josh was waiting outside when the convoy returned. He ran next to the driver's side of the first truck as it rolled in and said only two words.

"Martini, Sims?"

The driver understood. "They're bringing what pieces we could find. Sorry, man."

Josh felt the breath race out of his chest, staggered, and stood bent over in the road as the rest of the convoy maneuvered around him. He already knew, but the confirmation hit him hard. More buddies dead. Shit!

He decided not to tell Lucy about Martini. They Skyped a few more times before he left Afghanistan for his return home. He went forward, planning his future with Lucy, knowing that there would be no tomorrow for Martini and Sims. Lucy didn't make a big deal about the slight change in Josh's demeanor. Being a VA nurse, she did not miss much and understood that some things were better left alone. Josh would tell her about whatever it was when he was ready. Or not; she realized that he would have to be the one to make that call. Lucy did her best to reassure him without really knowing what the problem was. She felt stronger than ever about Josh's need for a decompression map. She knew a slow, hopefully fun, transition to civilian life was the best thing for him. It was the best thing she could do for their future.

Long after Josh returned home from Afghanistan he realized what Lucy had been up to while he was away. She and Dave's wife Linda had spent many evenings together talking and fixing up the new house. They would take turns waiting to hear the Skype ping that let them know Josh was calling in. Linda was good company for Lucy after the last bad bombing raid and getting disconnected.

"Keep your eyes on that screen Linda, while I finish painting this trim."

Linda sat with her glass of tea, eyes fixed on the screen. "How often can he Skype, Lucy?"

"It used to be about twice a week, but now I'm lucky if it's once. Thank God, he just has a couple more weeks before he comes home."

"I don't know how you do it. If I'd been able to communicate with Dave like this in Iraq, I would've gone crazy getting disconnected during a bombing raid."

"Each time, I just know he'll come home. I have to believe it. Besides, he'll be here soon. We're almost there!

"You've really given up a lot, letting Dave meet the plane. I must admit, I wish I'd thought of something like this for my hubby. He was so stressed when I first picked him up at Dover. We kissed, and then it was like he froze up for years. It lasted until he got help. You know the problems we've had."

Dave and Linda's experience was what Lucy wanted to avoid. They had both endured years of Dave's anger, therapy and maybe worse. "Yeah, and that's what gave me the idea. At least you guys got through it. He's doing great now. Maybe this'll help Josh."

Linda giggled and gave Lucy a wink. The bond between them had grown into a sisterhood. It was a relationship based on understanding and patience, born of their common experiences and their mutual desire for Josh's homecoming to be better than his brother's.

"Dave's so excited and grateful! He thinks you're the best for arranging all this, and so do I! If I'm going to watch paint dry and a blank screen, I need more ice tea."

Lucy raised her hand to stop Linda from leaving her seat. "I'll get it. Keep your eyes on the screen! I've never missed one of Josh's Skype calls, and I'm not about to start now. Considering I'm sending his brother and not me to pick him up, I don't want to miss even one chance to hear from him. He must already think I don't want him! Not really; Josh knows how excited I am. Still, please keep your eye on the screen."

As she refilled Linda's glass, Lucy turned around and saw everything the family had done to the inside of the house. Smiling, she imagined for a moment that Josh was standing in the doorway in his surf shorts.

Linda began to giggle, closing one eye and then the other while she watched the screen, "Thanks for the tea, and thanks for letting me know that I only need to use one eye. Now, if were a chameleon, I could be watching something else, too! Trust me, I'm sure not gonna be the one to miss his call. Neither of you would let me live that down! Josh is going to love this place."

"Yeah, we had so little time to look before he left. I really thought my dad had sold this old place for the real estate value. The building isn't much, but the land… When my dad told me I could buy it from him at cents on the dollar and we could build our life on the beach, I knew it was our dream come true! Kind of a late wedding present – a really big one! It's not exactly a mansion, but who cares?"

Both of them look out the open front door to the water view. Linda gives Lucy a funny look and tilts her head in amusement. "Lucy, it needs a lot—I mean a lot – of work, but it has a million-dollar beachfront!"

"Thanks, Linda! I know how much work it needs, but make that a five-million-dollar view! Thank God, Dad took it easy on us with the price and he takes payments!"

"Josh will go crazy over this place. When are you going to take down the sign?"

"I'm going to let him do that. He doesn't know my dad ever owned the property or anything about it. I used to come out here when I was a kid, but thought it was long gone. I hadn't thought about this land for years, until I was talking with my dad about looking for a starter home and mentioned that our dream was to one day live on the beach."

"Lucky you and lucky Josh! This is an amazing place, and no one can afford real estate like this anymore."

"We'll end up paying my dad exactly what he paid in the 1960's. It's not a big piece of beach, but it's ours. People can use it, but we live here and own up to twenty feet from the water's edge. There's a floating land boundary."

Linda jumped up from her chair, looking at her watch. "Look at the time! I have to run. The kids get out of school soon. How do you watch the screen when you're at the hospital or working around the house and I'm not here?"

"I have Skype set up to alarm for only Josh. I carry my laptop everywhere. Sometimes at the VA, I ask the vets in the waiting room to keep an eye on it. They hope he'll call while they're on guard duty. Everybody wants to say hi to him. Thanks for the help. I'll see you soon. Josh is almost home!"

"I can't believe that you talked Lois and Claude into waiting to see him!"

"I didn't talk them into anything. I just told them what I was thinking and why. They jumped right on board. His dad was all gung-ho about the map and it took his mom only a minute of thinking to agree. They loved the idea of Dave picking him up!"

"I know. They're great! Are your mom and dad coming to the barbeque after he gets here?"

"Heck yeah, they wouldn't miss it!"

"Okay, cool! I really do have to go. See ya later, Lucy!" They both hugged and Linda hurried, almost running, out the door. "Later!"

Over the next week, Lucy was busy fine-tuning her plans for the decompression map. Everyone in the family was involved in making suggestions and adjustments. Each one was based on intimate knowledge of Josh's likes and dislikes. Their collective memory served them well.

Lucy knew the plan for Josh was ready. The cool ocean breeze kissed her skin as she walked out the front door and took her usual place, sitting in one of two chairs on the beach, waiting and dreaming…

Matrix Filia & Claudette Walker

DECOMPRESSION

Matrix Filia & Claudette Walker

Los Angeles International Airport is crowded and loud as Dave arrives to pick up Josh. There are a mix of civilians and soldiers coming home, and more than a few waiting to leave. The sounds, announcements, and chatter melt into a background hum. After what seems like hours of waiting, he finally sees his little brother, still in fatigues. Dave begins jumping up and down, waving.

He calls out, "Josh! Josh!"

Josh spots him almost immediately, double-times it to Dave and grabs him in a bear hug. Josh utters only a single word, "Bro!" It is obvious that he is happy to be home and thrilled to see his brother. There is something more, too. Dave felt it when he returned from Iraq. It seems almost like relief, but it isn't – at least, not quite.

"Welcome home! God, you're a sight for sore eyes! Still in desert camos, too! Give me your rucksack – you've carried it far enough. It's time to see if I can still tote one of these things and hustle. We gotta get a move on." Together, they hurry through the throng of people headed toward the parking lot. "Lucy can't wait for me to get you home, and we have a whole bunch of things to do on the way!"

Josh laughs. "Lucy really did do it, didn't she, Dave? I wasn't really sure if she was serious or not. She got me to agree, and after that it was like a big secret. I thought she was pulling my leg. I mean a map? What a hoot! How is my girl?"

"She's great, excited, busy working on the house. She really did make a map for this trip, and you're gonna love it! My job is to drive." As they get out of the herd of people, Dave texts Lucy, "Got him." The cell phone dings almost immediately with Lucy's reply.

Dave hands the phone to Josh to read the text, "I love you! Enjoy the map!" A huge smile is on Josh's face as he tries to respond quickly. It takes a minute, because he has not texted in about a year. He is all thumbs and keeps hitting the wrong keys. "Told U I'd be home. LUV U!!!" Josh starts to dial Lucy as soon as he finishes texting.

Dave tells Josh to give back the phone. "No calling her yet! Step it up, soldier! We're wasting time! We need to get to the car."

"Shit, Dave, you knew what I was about to do! What's the rush? Heck, I've got all the time in the world. Besides, I'm all done with active duty – I don't have to take anybody's orders anymore!"

Dave flashes an almost evil grin. "I'm still your big brother, so I'm in charge here! As for why we're rushing, I want to beat the traffic out of this madhouse. Besides…well, you'll see!"

Josh suddenly stops in his tracks. Dave is still walking ahead and it takes him a few steps to realize that his brother is not moving. When he looks back, a tired, excited, yet scared Josh is looking at Dave as if they are kids again. "It's just you right? Promise, no one else is waiting?" He is nervous and fidgeting a bit. "I can't handle a whole crowd now."

Dave's eyes are misty. He understands what Josh is going through, because he has had the same feelings. The outcome for him was not so good. He wants better for his little brother.

"Hell no, Josh!" Then, more gently, "There's no crowd lurking in the parking lot. It's just me. I wouldn't do that to you, man! I know you feel like you're ready to explode. I promise it's just us and no one else." To lighten the mood Dave gives Josh a light hit on the shoulder. "But we have some fun in store. Here, Lucy sent your shades."

As Josh puts on his sunglasses, Dave laughs. "You can just chill, now that you're all Californ-i-a in your shades! You're home! They both laugh and return to walking towards the car. Dave is unable to hold in his excitement any longer and calls out, "Road trip!"

Josh is cheerful again. Dave knows the pressure is off – Josh has a little more bounce in his step and his voice is stronger. "Okay! Perfect!" He hurries ahead as he calls, "Let's move it, old man!"

"Who are you calling an old man? I can still whip your ass! 'Sides, I know where the car is, and you don't!" Dave sees Josh's excitement about being back home and remembers his own high spirits when he arrived from Iraq.

Josh yells out, "American soil! California!" Then more quietly, he continues. "There were way too many times I thought I'd never see her again!"

Dave smiles gently. "Man, I know that feeling! I felt the same way. Coming home sure does take on a whole new meaning when you damn near die!"

"Hell yeah, bro!" They head through the parking lot side-by-side, with Dave leading the way. His pace increases nearly to a run as they get closer to the car. Dave veers to the right, realizing that Josh is continuing straight ahead.

"This way – we're parked over here." Dave abruptly stops next to a gleaming convertible.

Josh halts in his tracks, thinking he is seeing a mirage. That happened to him sometimes in the desert. It must be an after-effect of the war. In complete disbelief, he points to the car, "This is Old Lucy? It can't be! Old Lucy was on her last legs; Luce told me she was afraid to drive to Dover in it!"

"Yes, this is your old car. Your wife lied. It was sitting in the driveway looking just like this when she told you that – we had a good chuckle! But it was a little white lie – she said that just so I had something to surprise you with."

Josh is clearly flabbergasted. "Oh my God, I can't believe this! Who? How? Man! Damn!"

Dave can't control his smile and laughter as he gets into the car, starts it up, and puts the top down. "I think you better just call her Lucy now! Everyone pitched in – Mom, Dad, Lucy – the whole family had a hand in it, and the guys at the body shop tossed in their labor. Welcome home! Get in!"

Josh jumps in the passenger's side and he runs his hands over the fragrant leather seat and the flawless dash in disbelief. For once, Josh is at a loss for words. Dave glows with pride. "Well, how did we do? Did we get it right?"

"Everything is perfect! Rocket red, leather, Bose, just what I planned. Wow, did you ever get it right!"

"Come on Josh, you only talked about restoring her for the last six years. Hell, I think you started planning the restoration the day you bought her! I heard it at least a hundred times; I remembered every detail I could. The shop knew some of the things you had talked about, so it should be spot on!" Josh leans over and hugs the dash, making a stroking motion and patting the top. He takes a deep breath and exhales, finally feeling like he is home. If this is a dream, he doesn't want to wake up. "It's perfect! This is way too much! Wow!"

Dave holds up a CD case and tosses it to Josh. "Even better, Dad sent music and I brought some. So we got tunes from the Doors and Warren Zevon to the Red Hot Chili Peppers. Pick your poison! You're in the co-pilot seat, so relax and enjoy the ride!"

They leave the airport on Sepulveda Boulevard and head north on the Pacific Coast Highway, Highway 1. Before long, mountains are all around and the ocean merges with the sky to their left. It always amazes Josh that some homes are built right into the cliffs, looking as if they will fall at any moment. He is glad that Lucy thought to send his shades – the sun is glistening off the water, and he does not want to miss a thing.

Dave tells Josh Lucy was relaxing on the beach with her computer, video cam, and cell phone next to her on a table when he texted her from the airport. The two brothers chat about how their parents are doing, and Dave tells him they are hanging out at the beach with Lucy.

In the weeks to come, Josh will be able to see what was going on at home while he was gone. Lucy has been taping it all. She has not missed a trick – she is even videotaping what is happening at the beach during his trip from L.A. She turns the phone so Josh's father, Claude, can read the text. He looks both excited and relieved. "Lois, our boy's home and I can breathe again!"

Lois, Josh's mother, grins at her husband's excitement. "Claude, Josh is safely with Dave and what a time they will have with Lucy's map!"

"Yes, they will!" Claude slaps his hand on his jeans. "Yep, Dave has him. I expect Josh will be on this beach in seventy-two hours or so. I'm not sure I can wait that long without busting!"

Lois laughs, "I think it'll be more like forty-eight. It doesn't matter; let them take their time together."

Lois and Claude approach Lucy sitting on the beach and Lois hugs her, "Lucy, this is so smart of you! It's hard to wait 'til Sunday to see our boy. But after what Claude and Dave went through, I'll go for anything that may make the transition easier for Josh."

Claude said with a smile, "Lucy, this is brilliant! I think you may have hit a home run with this one!"

"You really think so, guys? God, I hope so. Only time will tell. I just want Josh to have a moment to breathe. His brother seemed perfect for that."

Claude nodded as he hugged Lucy and Lois. "Dave's experiences were a lot more like Josh's than mine, so he was the right choice. Trust me, I've been where Josh is now, and I'm sure your idea is the best one I've ever heard for a homecoming.

"Will your mom and dad be here Sunday?" Lucy nodes her head and responds, "They wouldn't miss it, Lois!"

"Lucy, your parents really were lifesavers, letting you kids have this place. Weren't they

Claude?" He nods in agreement and stares at the house in pride. Even though it is only a shack on the beach, it is a much better place than when they started to their renovations. Besides, it has a multimillion dollar view of the ocean. "They sure did – this place is heaven on earth!"

"Well, my dad was sixty when I was born. It's like he said, he's too old to help with the work, so everyone's contributing. You both have done a ton to make it a home. And getting Old Lucy fixed – Josh must just be beside himself! I don't think I could ever thank you enough!" Lois and Claude are beaming, hugging each other.

Meanwhile, Dave and Josh are enjoying the seaside drive in "New Lucy." The top is down and wind is blowing a cool breeze. Dave is taking is easy, and Josh is soaking up the view and admiring every detail of his new old car.

Dave knows that the remainder of Lucy's map takes them northbound about a hundred miles or so, generally all on Highway 1, but he's not about to ruin the surprise for Josh. "Dave, I still can't believe this is my old car. The leather is so soft and the paint has clear coat! This is better than I could've dreamed. So, how much do we owe you guys?"

"The bill is paid, and we all agreed not to tell you. Everyone pitched in and the cost wasn't bad at all." Dave smirks as he tells his brother, "Oh, but I did tell the guys at the shop that you'd be sweeping floors for a long time to pay them back."

"That's fine with me! I think I owe everybody a lot more than that."

"I'm just screwing with you – the guys were happy to do it. They wanted to do something to welcome you back."

"Wow, thank you! I'll tell the guys in person – and somehow, I expect I'll be doing some volunteer work for them at the shop, too! Old – uh – New Lucy is simply unreal. I'm thrilled!" Josh tries the glove box but it is locked. "Got the key?"

"Lucy must have locked it."

"Okay, it's no big deal. I just wanna see every inch!"

Josh looks in the back seat to see a change of clothes Dave brought from Lucy. "Civvies! I guess that means it's official – I really am home!"

"Okay bro, start stripping! Lucy says all the way to your underwear. How 'bout a little Doors music?" Josh jumps into the backseat and starts to drum on the back of the front seat. He calls out, "Perfect start, a musical tribute to Dad's war."

"You got it bro! I'm thinking "Riders on the Storm."

"Hell, yeah!"

Josh changes into jeans, a Grateful Dead T-shirt, and sneakers. "Man, Lucy, sent my favorite jeans and T-shirt. Nice! There's a wallet in the pocket. Look, a picture of my Luce! Look at that red hair! Oh, and there's money, a cell phone, and a debit card; she didn't forget a thing! Even my old sneakers! These are the good old American ones. Now they're making 'em in China."

"Yeah, Dad returned a pair last month because they were made in Vietnam! The old man hasn't changed a bit! He looks pretty good for 62!"

"I'm glad to hear nothing much has changed. He always was a 'buy American' kind of guy."

"Josh, that Lucy's a real beauty and a great gal! She's the one who thought to come up with all this. I'll be honest, when you married her so fast after you met, the family thought you had lost your mind! Even though you were twenty-four, old enough to know, I guess. In the past year, we've really gotten to know her. She's nuts about you, and I tell her she's crazy for marrying your sorry butt! She sure is happy you're on your way home."

Josh whacks Dave lightly in the back of the head. "Thanks, Dave. Face it, when you have a red convertible named Lucy and a beautiful redhead named Lucy returns a $20.00 bill you dropped at Starbucks, it's gotta be a sign. We hit it off from the very beginning, and we both knew it was right"

Josh clambers into the front seat. "Okay, so where's this map?" Dave hands Josh the cell phone. "Pick up the phone and hit the one. It's not a traditional map, more like a journey."

"Cool!" Lucy pops up on Skype. She is clearly sitting on the beach. "Welcome home, baby! I see you found your clothes. That looks more like the man I married!"

"Lucy, I love you! The car looks great! I can't believe you guys did it. Just like I planned! Nice touch, my Grateful Dead T-shirt, shades, and the wallet too! Where are you, the beach?"

"Yes, I'm relaxing today, enjoying the sun. I'll be home when you arrive. I love you, too. Are you calling with the phone?"

"Yeah, why?

Dave suddenly jumps into the conversation, "Shit, Lucy! I got so excited seeing Josh, I forgot to get it out of the trunk. We'll call you back!"

Josh's has a puzzled look on. "Why?"

"Lucy knows. I'm pulling over now. Sorry! Hang up, Josh."

"No problem, Dave, at least you didn't forget Josh! Sorry honey, you missed another little surprise in all the excitement over the car."

"Really? What is it?"

"You'll see! Call me back in a minute."

"Okay. Bye."

The Skype call ends as Dave pulls into a scenic overlook on Highway 1. He jumps out and brings back two cases with iPads from the trunk. "Late Merry Christmas, bro! We both got one and they're set to go wireless. I was going to get them out at the airport, but I was so damn excited to see you, I forgot!"

"No shit! Wow! Too cool! Let me call her back." Josh calls Lucy back using his new toy, and she appears in a much larger picture. Lucy waves. "That's better! Now I can see you and your Grateful Dead T-shirt."

"Yeah, this is great!" Lucy quickly zooms so Josh can see less. He is looking at the background, trying to see clues to her location. Lucy is laughing. "I was afraid of that! Ha, I zoomed it in! Now the first stop is some real food for my baby. No more MREs for you! Call me again after you eat and tell Dave 'good job,' even if he did forget the iPad at the airport. At least he got the important part right. He got you!"

"Luce, you still haven't told me where we live."

Dave interjects, "Hey Lucy, I may have forgotten the iPads, but I haven't told him a damn thing. He can't pry shit out of me!"

Josh nodded his head vigorously. "I've tried all my tricks on him, and he won't tell me a thing. I guess that's because I learned all my tricks from him! Hon, can I at least know what town we live in?"

Lucy chuckled. "Nope!"

"Okay, I give! I'm in for the ride! Thanks for sending Dave to get me. I missed him the most next to you, and Mom and Dad too, of course."

"I know you missed him. Mission Retrieve Brother for a good time journey home is on! You two have not been on a road trip since before Dave went to Iraq, he told me. Besides, I'm busy with the house!"

"I'm sure it's wonderful. Baby, it's only a starter home. It'll be fine, don't worry. I'll love it 'cause you're there! Dave and I are having a great time. Old Lucy is running like new and man, is she pretty! About the house, what town did you say?"

Lucy shakes her finger at the screen. "Yeah, right! Love you!"

"Can't blame a guy for trying!"

"Love you sweetie; have fun. Bye!"

"Love you, Luce!

Dave is laughing as they head up the highway. "That wife of yours has everything planned. I'm gonna really catch hell if I break any of her rules."

"Don't worry bro, I don't want to mess this up. I'm just enjoying the hell out of this trip! How are Linda and the kids?"

"They're great. The kids just keep growing like weeds. Man, are they excited to see you." Josh leans his seat back a bit to enjoy the sky. "This is the best you know, just the two of us. How long since we took a road trip together? Lucy said it was before you left for Iraq. It had to be years ago. I was still a kid."

"Yep, it was before I deployed. Nobody could stand to be around me for long after I got back. I was a real asshole to everyone, including you. I'm sorry."

"Yeah, you sure were! But that's in the past. Back then, I didn't get it, but I understand it more now. We're together and it's our road trip. Let's do it!"

Josh and Dave both scream out in unison, "Road trip!" as the car makes its way up the highway. Queen's Bohemian Rhapsody is playing loudly over the new stereo system.

Within a few minutes, Dave takes a side road and pulls into a McDonald's drive-through. The intercom lady greets them. "May I take your order, please?"

"Oh man, just what I wanted, two Quarter Pounders, large fry, two apple pies, and a huge Dr. Pepper! Ketchup, please."

"Make that two."

Josh looks at Dave, "Afghanistan is a dry fucking place."

"Yeah, so was Iraq! Too few condiments in the war zone, too!"

"Right. After all, isn't ketchup a vegetable?"

As the car pulls away, Josh starts eating a sandwich. Dave pulls over to the ocean side of the road. They get out and sit on a rock in front of the car as they eat. Dave takes a minute between bites to ask Josh, "Well, is war hell, like I told you?"

"You said nothing could prepare me for it. You were right. It really was death and mayhem with moments of terror-filled silence. Your description was perfect. I'll never forget it!"

Dave reaches for his soda. "I take it you had the misfortune to hear the quiet just before all hell breaks loose. Did you go on high alert?"

"I got that one down pretty fast! Saved my ass many times! The last time, Martini and I were on patrol the day I got my stick. The silence was petrifying, so we ran a scan of the area and picked up insurgents to the north getting ready to hit the convoy. I called in live fire, no foss, and we all made it out alive!"

"Fuck, that's a hard call! Over your head?"

"Damn right, over the whole convoy!"

"Shit! I bet there were some dirty drawers at the end of that run! Wow, that didn't come out well."

As their laughter faded, Dave got quiet. "The stuff we've gone through, man. I'm shocked that either of us made it back alive. You know, when I came back from Iraq, I felt no one understood what I'd seen. I never want you to feel that way."

Josh has a faraway look. "I've had nightmares for a while. I've even created giant robots in my mind to fight and win the battles in my dreams!"

"The robots are a nice touch – I hadn't thought of that one! But the nightmares, they'll taper off in time. Just remember, you have to control the battles. You gotta win in the dreams. When you wake, the war won't be there, and you'll be alive. People don't realize self-preservation allows us to control our thoughts to a certain degree."

Josh nodded. "You told me that before I left. I didn't understand the importance then. Once the nightmares started, I remembered you said your psychiatrist had talked with you about it. I told Lucy about the dreams, and we worked through it. She's was great."

"She really is. Linda and I went to the VA for lunch and I saw her in action."

"I'm glad you guys are getting close."

"So, going back to what you said, you mean we don't have giant robots in the military arsenal yet?" Dave laughs out loud at his own question, "Damn, I thought they would've by now."

"No not for land, just the air drones. Those are pretty damn nice!"

They are taking their time eating, watching the ocean, and talking. "Man, is this good. Better than the rations I've been eating! That's just whining about the MREs; the food wasn't really that bad. But everything I ate was coated in sand!"

"Yeah, ours wasn't too horrible either, but the limited choice is a killer. How much fruit cocktail did you eat? I'd have gotten you a steak, but Lucy... she insisted on McDonald's."

"No, this is perfect! I told her I was jonesing for a Quarter Pounder! Yeah, fruit cocktail – I ate way too much! Traded it for peaches when I could."

During most of the time the brothers are traveling, Lucy is on the beach in one of two chaises, looking back again toward the road and smiling at the thought of where the guys are on the map and what they are doing. She sips her tea and laughs aloud at the thought of the two brothers decompressing.

Dave places Josh's camouflage uniform inside the trunk and pulls out their two ball gloves and a baseball. They play catch on the ocean's edge as they talk. "Tell me about the new house. Lucy won't give up a thing!"

"No way! Lucy would kill me. All I'll tell you is that you'll love it. Now, no more questions like that."

"Come on, Dave! Give me something – I'll like it, right?"

"That's all I'm gonna say!"

Josh surrenders to his brother, "Okay, okay, I get it. I know you're sworn to silence. Man, it feels so strange being home. With Iraq over and Afghanistan about to wind down, it looks like I'm out for good."

With a snicker Dave asks, "Don't wanna re-up?"

"Hell no! I'm subject to recall, but I have no intention of voluntarily going back!"

"What was the country like in Afghanistan, besides hot, dry, and dangerous?"

"It's mostly rugged mountain terrain, cold in the winter, hot in the summer. There's also a bunch of desert, thrown in just for fun. Potable water is in short supply. Poppy fields are all over, and yet it's dirty and poverty-ridden. Somebody's making money, but it's not the ordinary people."

Dave nods, "Sounds like Iraq. The Iraqis used their drug profits to buy weapons. Did you try any opium while you were there?"

"Nope! Took your advice – I stayed clean. I remember you saying the only way out of war was straight through on high alert. So I stayed sober and didn't smoke any of their shit! Opium has a hell of a good smell, though!"

"Josh, listen to me. I need to be serious with you for a minute. Post-traumatic stress disorders are the invisible wounds of war. It will be easy for you to overlook the signs. Dad and I did that for a long time. Learn from our mistakes. We want to be here for you because we don't want you losing years of your life to the bottle or worse. All three of us were soldiers on patrol, kicking down doors, dodging IED's or bouncing Betties, making sorties, and manning check points. From the jungles where Dad was to the deserts we were in, it's all the same. Death is always right around the corner. You and I both know what we've seen in war. PTSD happens gradually. It's like carrying logs; they just keep piling up on you until you drop. You've got to stay close to us, and for God's sake, speak up! We can help you through this."

"Watch me close and if you or Dad see any signs, talk to me please. I promise you this, I won't get angry. I want to put this behind me, not have it rule and ruin my life."

"You mean angry like the old man and I did when anyone tried to talk to us?"

"Yeah exactly like that! No offense, but I don't want the history you have with Linda to become the fate of Lucy and me. I know your marriage barely survived. Hell, you barely survived the bottle!"

"No offense taken. You're right. My binge drinking almost killed me in that motorcycle accident. I ran the bike ten feet up a chain link fence, drunk as a skunk. Damn near died. Fucking binge drinking! Drink 'til you pass out or you're so drunk that you think you're immortal. That night opened my eyes and got me into treatment. Damn lucky to be alive. Did you suffer any head trauma in Afghanistan that you blew off?"

"Probably, but nothing comes to mind. Only thing I can really think of is that once during a bombing near camp when I was on the perimeter, a blast tossed a bucket up in the air. It hit the side of my head and knocked me to the ground. I did feel dazed for a while, but it was nothing." Dave looks hard at Josh, "Yeah, we shake off a lot as warriors. Okay, we'll watch close, and if we see any signs, we'll have you checked for traumatic brain injury first and then go from there."

"Thanks, but I'm fine... I hope I'm fine."

"We're going to make sure of it! We all made it back alive; now we want to be certain your brain is okay and your head's on straight. Don't want a repeat performance with you!"

"I hear you, Dave!"

"Come on, it's time to Skype Lucy."

Back in the car, Josh picks up the iPad and calls Lucy. She pops up on the screen all smiles. "Well, how was your burger?"

"Which one? I had a couple. They were amazing and as perfect as my jeans. I'm home! Yes, I'm really home!"

"You are, baby! How's the trip? Are you relaxing with your brother?"

"We're having a great time!"

"Good! That's what this is all about. I love you. Tell Dave it's time for location two. Later, boys!"

Dave answers. "I can hear you Lucy! I'll proceed forward as commanded!"

Lucy laughs. "I forgot you can hear and see me, Dave! Have fun!"

They end their call and continue up the highway. Dave then takes a turn and heads into a strip center off a side road. He pulls the car into a parking space in front of Starbucks, gets out, and begins walking a few stores down to a surf shop.

As he starts to walk, he looks over his shoulder to his brother. "Surf's up! I need to run into Manny's for just a minute, Josh. Wait here, I'll be right back. Unless you want to come in, too."

"No, I'll stay in the car. Wish we had our boards, but renting 'em is cool. Just so we can hit some waves." While Josh waits, he looks around and tries out the radio. Within moments, he sees Dave emerging from the shop with two surfboards. "Lucy's idea?"

"Of course! Come on! Get our suits from the trunk."

"Hey, that's my board! How did she do that?"

"Well, it started like this, according to what Lucy told me. Lucy was talking with Manny, who owns the surf shop, about your decompression trip. She's known him since they were kids. When she told him about the plan, he offered to help. He told her he would hold the boards for us. I met him when Lucy and I came down yesterday. He said you were one lucky guy to have gotten their Lucy!

"He knew you might or might not come in with me today. In a few weeks, she's going to have some friends over to meet you. Manny said to tell you 'Welcome home,' and he'd be waiting for his invite."

Manny steps out front of the shop, then nods and waves to Josh. "Do you think I ought to go over and thank him?"

"Nah, he told me he knew what it's like – he said a wave back was fine with him."

As Josh gets out of the car and waves to Manny, Dave tells him, "Nice guy. He told me he was doing it for you, Lucy, country, and for every surfer who loves his own board!"

They jump into their wetsuits at the changing station and head out into the ocean. The waves are crashing hard, but Josh manages to get on his board and ride it toward shore, "It's just like the old days. The waves are great, but I think I'm a little rusty!"

Dave calls back, "Lucy ordered special waves, too!"

Josh screams at the top of his voice, "I'm home! Bring it on!"

Dave replies, "Yes, you are!"

Feel it, the surf gods are alive today, Dave!"

"Yeah, and so are you!"

As they return to the car, they grab towels and their clothes. Dave suggests catching a few winks in the car before they call Lucy. "Then we can grab coffee for the road. Starbucks is right here."

"Sounds good, I could use a nap! I dreamed of that water every night. Well, at least I did when I wasn't on patrol, getting shot at or having nightmares!"

They both lay back and rest on the car seat, catching the sun on their faces as they close their eyes. Dave doesn't sleep much; he just watches his brother and the clock on his phone.

Josh wakes after only a short nap, startled. With a sudden jerk, he sits upright in his seat, pushing his back against the car door. Dave is careful not to touch him, and speaks soothingly, "Josh, it's Dave. You're home. It's all right, you're home."

"Man! I was sure I was still there."

"You okay?"

"Yeah I'm fine, just a little freaked."

"This is going to happen to you for a while, on and off."

"I know. It just took a second to realize I was here, but that second was a doozy."

"Well, you are home now, and before you close your eyes to sleep, remind yourself of that. It may help."

"I'll try that."

"Sure you're okay?"

"Yes, I was just glad to see your mug! I'm good."

Dave glances at his watch. "Let's get that coffee now."

They walk into Starbucks in the mid-afternoon. There are only a few people inside as they head to the counter. Josh recognizes the place and excitedly says, "Dave, this is where I met Lucy! Nothing has changed. We sat at that table and talked for hours. Then we got married two weeks later. That blew everybody's mind!"

"You sure did surprise us! She told us all about it. Still take it black?"

"Yep, large, black, and strong! It was busy when we pulled in, but it's quiet now." Josh is looking around.

Dave winks at his brother, "I thought it would be better after the lunch crowd left and we hit the waves."

"I'll get a seat. Inside or out?"

"You pick. I'm just the tour guide."

"Out."

The patio is fairly quiet with the exception of a few people chatting at tables. "So, how are you really doing, Dave?"

"I'm great. I'm still working at FGI. The company has grown a lot in the last year. Video games are booming. My tech skills keep me employed. When you're ready, if you want, there's a job opening for someone with your skills. I'm sure you're even better with the joysticks than me. You know, you also have GI benefits, if you want more college."

"No way! My BA is enough. I don't want to study that hard again! Besides, I'm a married man now, and the parties just wouldn't be as interesting anymore."

"I understand." Dave gives Josh a slight smile. "By the way, I'm still not binge drinking – two drinks, no more. It's been over two years since I tied one on."

"Congratulations! That's good to hear, Dave. I'm gonna stick to your plan – two drinks, and no more. Two years! Wow!"

"Well, two years and eleven months actually. I'm still designing game software at work, and it's a blast, keeps me focused!"

"Heck, I'm definitely interested in a job! Mom and Dad – how are they?"

"Mom keeps Dad exercising and he still forgets to set up the coffee. Their health is good. My kids are doing great. Lilly is 12 going on 18 and Abe is still a bookworm."

"Dave, I have no idea what Lucy paid for the house, but she said it was cheap by California standards. She also said it's pretty run down, but we can get a start there and the seller carried the paper. Where is it?"

"Josh, don't worry about the house. She had your back on this one!"

"Okay, good. Lucy and I decided we are going to wait a while to have kids; we want to travel some first."

"Good idea! Lucy has been great about enlisting Dad's help with the new house. It keeps him out of Mom's hair! They both adore her. If your marriage doesn't work out, they're keeping her and you're screwed!"

Josh starts laughing. "I'll be sure it works out – no way I'm losing a bride and my family, too! So Dave, about that new house. Can't you just give me a few clues?"

"Ain't happening, brother! Time to move on! Let's go!"

The car heads out of the parking lot and Josh notices they need gas. "Pull in here. Lucy's getting low on gas, and I got money to burn, thanks to my other Lucy!"

"Got it."

Josh points to an open pump, and Dave pulls up to it. The brothers get out and Josh begins to look around.

Dave with a laugh says, "I don't think pumps have changed since you left. Fill 'er up!"

"Does she still drink gas? Wow, look at the price!"

"Not as bad as she did before the overhaul. I know, gas prices have changed a lot since you left."

"No shit!"

"Unreal, huh?"

"Yeah, Lucy put cash in my wallet, so I'll pay. I have a little in my duffel bag too, if we need it. Sign says I gotta pre-pay." Josh starts for the station to pay and Dave immediately tells him, "I'll go with you. I want some chips."

Josh seems amused. "Come on Dave, you don't want chips, you're being careful about the number of people I'm exposed to. Let's see, you rushed me out of the airport, a drive-thru and not a restaurant, a quiet part of the beach, and you waited 'til after lunch when the coffee bar was less crowded – it was packed when we first got there. I remember my debriefing: don't kill anyone. I'm okay – in fact I'm just fine!"

"That's the same thing they told me. Don't kill anyone! Not a whole lotta help! It's true, I'm easing you back in, but it's Lucy's plan, so don't blame me."

Josh becomes momentarily serious. "I'm calming down a lot. I was really wound up on the plane. Lucy understands what's going on. I suppose I oughta just go with the program. After all, it's worked, so far." Then he was back to jovial. "Come on – let's get your chips. Then I suppose it's about time to Skype Luce?"

"Mind-reader, my little brother's a freakin' mind-reader!"

After gassing up and getting some chips, they head back on the road and make the call. "How were the waves?"

"Sweet baby, real sweet! Honey, you have everything planned. God, I love you!"

Dave chirps in. "Oh boy, that lovey-dovey talk will fade with the years."

Lucy shakes her finger jokingly. "Dave, would you like me to tell Linda that? I can call her."

"Sorry Lucy, I'll be good."

"Remember, all you are doing is bringing Josh safely home to my arms, with a little fun thrown in for good measure!"

Josh is grinning. He thinks how great it is to see the interaction between his wife and brother; he can tell what good friends they have become. "I love the map, sweetie. I love you, and what a brother!"

Lucy's computer camera moves from view for a moment, "I have someone on the ladder here who wants to say hello...

Josh's father Claude appears in the picture. "Hello son, welcome home!"

"Dad, how are you?"

"I'm great! You're home! Lucy claims she needs our help at the house, so she's been keeping Mom and me busy. Are you having a good time with Dave?"

"We're having a great time. Still striking that Zippo with both hands?"

"I've been striking it with my right hand for good luck the entire time you've been gone. Now, I need to see if it worked. Show me all your limbs!" Josh passes the iPad to Dave, who holds it in one hand as Josh waves his legs and arms in the front seat of the car, "See!"

Dave can't control his laughing now, "He looks like a nut flailing his arms and feet in the convertible!" Dave hands the iPad back to Josh.

"That's okay - I don't give a hoot what other people think of my kid. I wanted to see all Josh's appendages, just to be sure. Same shit, different war!"

"Dad, you look wonderful! Is Mom there, too?"

Lois appears onscreen. "Hello baby! I'm so happy to see your home. I'm lining the cabinets at you're new house!"

Josh tries to get more information about the house, but his mother is as adept as Lucy and his brother at warding him off. "Is that Linda in the background?"

Linda appears on the screen. "Welcome home, Josh!"

"Where are the kids?"

"They're at Little League practice. I'll be picking them up in a while."

Now Lois is back onscreen, as Josh tries again to see the house. "Mom, can you turn the monitor a little so I can see you better?"

"No way! Now you really don't think you can fool me into spoiling the surprise! I love you, but I'm not stupid! You boys be careful. We'll see you Sunday!"

Lucy appears back on the screen. "Sneaky, Josh! Yes, I would say you are a lucky man. Okay, tell...

Dave says, "Lucy, I'm in the same car. Just because you can't see me doesn't mean I can't hear you and see you...."

Josh interrupts. "So, love of my life, what do you have in store for me now?"

"Oh, I keep forgetting, Dave! Number three, find an old lady and help her. We all love you, Josh. Bye!" The call ends.

"What? You've gotta be kidding! Haven't I done enough for this country?"

"Yes you have, Josh. I don't know why, but Lucy thinks this is important. She knew you'd object – notice how fast she hung up?"

"I can't believe you'd do this to me! Hell, I'm your little brother. You're supposed to be on my side!"

Dave is laughing hysterically. "Don't bitch to me, I'm just the driver! You agreed to Lucy's plan. I'm just following orders! If you're gonna blame anybody, blame yourself. You're the one who went along with this map thing!"

Josh sighs. "I know, I know, but I oughta be able to vent a little to you! Isn't that part of why you're here? Mom and Dad do look great!"

"Trust me, they're fine, in good health and as spunky as ever! Mom's been worrying since you deployed. Dad, well he doesn't let on to her how worried he's been. But we talked. We were all scared to death. Man, I'm glad you're back"

"I'm glad to be here!"

"Josh, you know Dad and I were both young when we went to war. You were twenty-four. We couldn't decide whether it was better to go when you're too young and dumb to be afraid or when you're old enough to understand the danger. We finally agreed it sucks at any age. Only thing is, because we were so young, I want to know what you think."

"You're right, it sure did suck! I thought I understood the danger. But even at my age, I had no real feel for just how bad it would be. It's not something you can be ready for, no matter how old you are. I guess the only way anybody could really get it at the beginning would be if they'd been in combat before."

"Well, thank God you'll never have to find that one out! I don't think you will be headed back."

"Damn right!"

They drive into a small town with a sign saying, "Saltwater Creek." Dave parks on the main street, not far from a bakery.

"What's up? Saltwater Creek? Never heard of it. Why are we stopping here?"

"This is where I chill with your Bose and you have to find an old lady to help." Dave tunes the CD player, lays back and crosses his arms in the car.

"Only Lucy would come up with this one! I don't see any old ladies. Everybody I see is under 30, and most of 'em look younger than me!"

"Well, you better look around real hard, 'cause this car stays parked until you find one. Your wife's orders!"

Josh throws his hands up, laughs as he gets out of the car, and starts to walk and look. "Okay, Okay!" There is not a soul on the street over 30 years old. After a few minutes, he sees a lady through a bakery window and motions to his brother, who laughs. He goes inside.

A lady pushing sixty-five years old asks, "May I help you?"

"Yes, hi. My name is Josh, and my wife has me on a mission as part of a map quest. Assisting someone is on the list of things I need to do. Can I help you with anything? Maybe sweep your floor or something?"

The lady smiles, then with a slight chuckle she says, "I'm Martha Gibson. It's nice to meet you, Josh. I'm sure I can find something. That idea you had of sweeping sounds like a good one to me. Here's a broom. Thank you, I mean, please thank your wife for me."

Josh takes the broom and begins cleaning. After a few minutes of silence he says, "I'm just coming home from Afghanistan. My wife sent my brother to pick me up with a decompression map for us to follow. I haven't been home yet. I'm still on my way. She thought I needed to ease back into civilization before I get hit with all the day-to-day routine."

Martha seems pleased that Josh has decided to talk. "Welcome home, son! A decompression map! That's something I never heard of! I'll get some cookies for you. Keep that wife of yours, she's a smart lady! I guess that's your brother, out there in the convertible laughing."

They peek out the window and see Dave sitting in the car. "Yeah, that's my brother, Dave. He's getting a real kick out of watching me work. When we were kids, seeing my big brother laughing at me working would have driven me nuts. Now, we're older and I hope I'm a little wiser. Besides, I'm so glad to be here, I don't think anything could bother me a whole lot. Thank you for letting me help."

Martha's eyes are misty as she tells Josh, "Son, you've done more to help me than you know. You're doing much more for me than just sweep a floor. Thank you." Martha points to a Marine soldier's photo on the wall behind the counter, "Katie's my daughter. She died in Yusfiyah, Iraq, two years ago come May. A convoy of trucks and soldiers were making their way up the dirt road. A Humvee with my Katie and another soldier hit an IED and they were killed. A radio operator heard Katie talking about Ashley, her daughter, and me just before they hit the mine." The woman is visibly upset, but trying to be strong.

"It meant a lot to know her thoughts were with us when it happened. The radio operator who overheard Katie called me a few months later. He said that he heard her say, 'Who thought they would use a thirty-seven year old reservist in war?' He told me she was talking about the bakery and how glad she was I had her daughter Ashley. Seems even the other soldier was talking about my cookies right before they hit the mine. Katie had just told him that I had more on the way. Well, I hope some soldier got them." She sits for a moment to collect her thoughts, but still seems distant.

Josh, stunned by what he has walked into, responds to the death of Mrs. Gibson's daughter. "I'm so sorry. I hope I haven't upset you! Too many have died in the war; I'm just a lucky one. I'm really sorry."

"Thank you hon, but it's just the opposite. Seeing you come home is a gift. It's not upsetting to me at all. You're one of the lucky ones. You came home alive and unhurt. I'm so happy you came into the bakery! If she had to die, at least my Katie didn't linger. They say her vehicle took a direct hit and she didn't suffer at all. I really hope that's true."

Josh feels like he was meant to be with her at this very moment. "Mrs. Gibson, I know that's right. I've seen it happen. She would not even have heard it coming." Martha smiles through light tears.

"I find some comfort in that and lots of joy in my granddaughter, Ashley!"

A young woman wearing fatigues walks out from the back of the bakery. "Oh, here she is now. Josh, this is my granddaughter, Ashley. She leaves for Afghanistan tomorrow. I'm petrified for her! Do you have any advice? After all, you just got back, so you know what's up over there."

"Hello, I'm Ashley." She comforts her grandmother, "Nana, you don't need to worry, I'll come home to you."

He was right. This was his purpose. "Can I give you a few tips you won't read in the travel brochures?"

"I'll take anything you've got."

"Always look to your left and right when driving the mountain terrain. Watch out for IEDs, 'cause they're all over! A year of war is nine months of boredom with three months of sheer terror thrown in for effect! It comes as a mix and you never know what day will be terror-filled. Be careful and stay low. Get to know your communication operators so you can call home. The comm folks can sometimes hook you up, so it pays to be nice to them. Here, let me write my Skype ID and phone number down. Call me anytime. I mean it – anytime. Remember; don't trust anyone who comes at you quickly, whether it's a man, woman, or even a child."

Martha interjects, "Why don't you two talk more while I get some cookies ready to go. After all that sweeping, I expect you could use a few, and your brother looks like a guy who might want to help you with a snack." Martha goes through the door to the back room of the bakery while Josh and Ashley sit down at a table.

"What's your assignment, Ashley?"

"I'm going to be assigned to fresh water duty. That seems pretty simple; just getting water for the camp."

Josh's face cannot hide his concern for her. "Ashley, I don't want to scare your grandmother. But don't trust any locals in burkas. You can't assume anyone is safe. They carry things under robes. Anyone could be inside a burka, 'cause they're completely covered. It could be a man or a woman, and maybe with a gun or a bomb. Stand them off a hundred feet or more with your rifle in one hand and stick your other hand up for them to stop. Call out stop, stop. They'll understand you, even if they don't speak any English. If they keep coming, you have to shoot 'em. If you don't shoot, they could kill you and everyone else within a hundred feet"

"I understand - anything else?"

"Some of the tribes use women and kids as weapons, 'cause they know we try not to hurt non-coms. And they'll steal uniforms off the dead, so that you think they're friendlies. Just stay on high alert. From the day you arrive to the day you leave, you'll need to keep your guard up. Don't try the opium. I can tell you, it smells really good. But you always need to be straight, and smoking it will dull your senses. You can't afford to relax; even a little inattention can cost you your life and the lives of your buddies. The fresh water duty you pulled is real dangerous. Be on guard, shoot first and ask questions later. That's the best way to make it out alive."

Ashley nods in understanding. "How do the guys treat woman soldiers in a war zone? I haven't had it too bad so far, but I don't know what it's like over there."

"In my unit, we treated them just like sisters. You've already seen it stateside. It's no different as far as my unit. You'll catch the same shit as everybody else, but you won't get any extra just because you're female. Just pull your weight and you'll be fine there. Keep your head down, and remember to stay on high alert!"

The aroma of fresh baked cookies flows through the air and breaks the tension of the conversation. Martha brings some cookies to Josh and gives him a huge hug. She laughs when she looks outside. Through the window, she sees Dave sniffing the air hungrily, and points him out to Josh. They all say their goodbyes.

"Ashley, you'll be okay. Semper Fi! Remember, call me whenever you want." Martha and Josh walk out of the front door of the bakery and onto the sidewalk.

"Mrs. Gibson, thank you for letting me help out in the bakery, and thanks so much for the cookies."

"No, thank you for coming in. You have given me comfort in the death of Katie, and more importantly, I know whatever you told Ashley will increase her chances of safely coming back to me. Thank you."

"Goodbye, Mrs. Gibson."

"Goodbye Josh. Please come see me again."

"I will, I promise."

Josh is heading to the car with a big box of cookies and a look of distress on his face. Dave is laughing as Josh passes the cookies to him while he gets in the car. "Very good, and you brought me goodies!" As he speaks, Dave notices the look on Josh's face. "Dave, have you been to this bakery before?"

"No, never heard of this beach town until Lucy told me about it, but the cookies look great! It was priceless to watch you sweep that floor, I laughed my ass off."

"I saw you, and so did Mrs. Gibson!"

"Are you okay?"

"That woman lost her daughter in Iraq a couple of years ago, and her granddaughter is a Marine, leaving for Afghanistan tomorrow. Goddamn, it doesn't stop!"

Dave is stunned by what Josh walked into when he entered the bakery. "Shit, Josh! I had no idea."

"Ashley, the kid, is going into the fresh water unit. They give the most dangerous jobs the sweetest names."

"You bet. Same in Iraq. In the damn desert, they'll kill you for water or try to poison it. At least we're out of Iraq, but we're still in Afghanistan. I'm sure it's the same there. I hope she makes it home all in one piece. The IEDs have taken many a soldier's limbs and worse. Man, I'm sorry for Ashley and her grandma. There's no way to prepare someone for what's coming."

"You're right. I couldn't explain to that kid what she's heading into. I hope she'll be okay. I gave her a few tips, my contact info, and told her to call. Seemed like the least I could do. Now they are moving the American women into these combat positions. We had a Brit, Sims, attached to our unit."

"I guess that makes sense, Josh. After all, we're on the same side, so we might as well fight in combined units. Did you pray in Afghanistan?"

"Yep! You know what they say; there are no atheists in foxholes or in the Afghan mountains! I would have made a deal with the devil if it got me out alive. In fact, I think I did. But don't worry, I'm reneging!"

"Well, we weren't raised religious, but I decided in Iraq it couldn't hurt to pray."

"Damn right, I prayed get me home to my redhead every night!"

"Well, we made it back. Someone or something in the universe heard our prayers!"

"Either that or we just got lucky. I don't have the answer to that one! Let's get moving."

Dave drives out of Saltwater and heads up the highway. Josh is quiet for a few minutes as he stares at the ocean before he turns to his brother, "Have you completely put Iraq behind you?"

"Nope, never will. No more than you'll ever put Afghanistan completely out of your mind. It's part of us forever. It's just not the controlling part of me anymore. For way too long after I got back, it was in control, I wasn't. There's a part of me that'll always remember, forever. Like when Goldman came to relieve me at a checkpoint in Al Kahaji."

"What happened?"

"I remember like it was yesterday. I was headed to the chow tent and didn't get more than a hundred feet away when I was knocked to the ground by a blast at the checkpoint. During the changing of the guard, I was leaving and Goldman was taking over, checking people passing into the Green Zone. I said, 'Thanks, Goldman; my feet are killing me! It's been pretty silent around here today, so keep a close eye out. It's just been too quiet to suit me.' Goldman said, 'You always say that, and nothing ever happens! Smith, the chow's hot. I got the check point.' I told him, 'Yeah hot, like everything else in this Godforsaken place!' Then I walked toward the tent. I heard Goldman call out, 'Let them through, let them through.' I was about a hundred feet away. Only two groups went through the checkpoint after I walked away. Suddenly, a blast knocked me to the ground. I got up quickly, I think. There was chaos all around me. Goldman and others at the checkpoint were killed by a bomb."

The brothers ride in an eerie silence for a moment before Dave continues, "A boy strapped with a bomb took out Goldman and six other soldiers, plus a bunch of non-coms. All of them fucking died."

Josh looks at his brother. "I'm sorry about Goldman and the others, but shit, you were lucky!"

"Yeah, real fucking lucky. These days, I try only to remember my buddies and the nice people I met. There were lots of good people just trapped in a war zone. Those were the ones I tried to help. And I want to remember the country more than the ones who were lost or killed. But they're all still there in my head. We had suicide bombers who were just little kids. I expect you saw the same thing. That's the worst."

"Tell me about it. Our satellite Humvees are major targets for them. A bunch of suicide bombers died without ever putting a dent in my truck. Sometimes it was 'cause their bombs just weren't strong enough, and sometimes it was our good shooting. Mostly, it was pure luck. We're still waiting for the MRAPs, the new safer vehicles. They were promising them when I arrived, and they were still saying they were on the way when I left."

"So let me guess – they never arrived?"

"Hell no. Not to us. Lots of bombs succeeded with trucks that were less armored than the comm Humvees. Damn contractors are selling the government faulty equipment or installing good equipment badly. They'd promise lots but didn't produce. Those assholes cost a lot of lives."

Josh stirs, angry, "Half the scopes we got didn't work! They'll wait until the war's over and then turn some kind of crap in. No one will notice until the next war!"

"By now, you must know that war is big money. It's something you'll never forget, Josh. The good news is I hear the contracts for the

MRAPs have gone out to a bunch of new contractors now and they have multiple assembly lines building them."

"I'll believe it when I hear they got 'em!"

"Me too! It may just be wishful thinking. The contractors were so bad in Iraq that we got electrical shocks when we turned on the damn shower taps they installed!"

"Well, it was a really good day in our camp when we heard we got Bin Laden. These jihadists claim to be fighting a holy war. Really, it's just profiteers, hate mongers, opium producers, and other scumbags behind it. They manipulate the poor and uneducated. We went on high alert about four hours before the raid. No patrols and radio silence. We didn't know exactly what was up but knew something was happening. Scary night."

"Josh, more men have been killed in the name of God than any other. When we got Bin Laden, I knew these wars would wind down and you would be coming home. Things will settle until the next war monger ignites conflict somewhere in the world in the name of God, hatred, money, or power."

"For sure. They light the fire and thousands die. At least we got a ton of intel on Al Qaida in that raid. That was all the talk at the camp – the intel!"

"Josh, did you know the President was at a press club dinner just before the attack? He kept a straight face the entire time, knowing it was about to happen. The whole time, he knew that the Seals were on their way."

"Oh man, we heard it a few days later and laughed our asses off. I sure wouldn't want to play poker with him. If he'd just dropped a bomb, we'd have never gotten the intel or known for sure if Bin Laden was dead. That SOB killed over three thousand people just in the World Trade Center. His guys hit the Pentagon, and he was behind thousands more deaths in America, the United Kingdom, and other parts of the world!"

"Well, at least those people in the plane over Pennsylvania had a chance to fight back and saved the White House."

"Hey, remember the week before I left for Afghanistan?"

"Yeah, I was ready to knock you out and tie you down – anything to keep you from going! I was so damn scared I would never see you again. You're a bookworm, like my boy. I didn't think you were a warrior, but hell, war makes us fighters."

"For three days, you tried to convince me that we could trade places and get away with it! You said that they barely look at the ID of a soldier bound for a war zone. Hell, they know no one wants to go. You told me that nobody but you would be crazy enough to pretend to be a soldier and get on a plane going into a war zone. So they would have just assumed you were me."

"Well, was I right?"

"Yes, I was sent straight to the zone, and they barely looked at my orders or my ID. I often thought we could've gotten away with it! You were sure that our names would work – you were even grateful for the first time that Mom and Dad named us David Joshua and Josh David."

"See, you should've listened to your big brother. I was trained, and they'd never have figured it out."

"Yeah, by the third day of you hounding me, I knew you were dead serious about going in my place. They did a summary check of my ID once from Dover to Afghanistan. You had it all figured out, laminate your picture on my ID. Can't say I didn't think about it for a minute. I knew you could shoot, but map reading and calling in strikes? Well, I'm not so sure about that."

"Shit, I'd have been a quick study and called in strikes all over. I just never wanted you to go through war; I'd already done it. I just knew what you were headed for – figured I could do it again and you would never go through what dad and I had. Three generations, three wars. It's just too much to ask of any family!"

"Dave, I was determined to make it home and thank you for that. If I ever doubted you, it ended that day."

"Oh hell, Josh, I just wanted one more fight. You know the warrior in me! Dad would have understood—he did 'Nam. He still talks about pumping up his body when they got near a tunnel hole in Vietnam so they'd think he was too big to go down! And about when he had to jump into the Han River and his buddy Porter didn't make it."

"Yeah, dad's buddy Porter…"

"Josh, this trip may help you relax some coming in, but your combat experiences are gonna be right up front in your head for a while. They'll never disappear, but it gets easier. I'm here for you and so is Dad. We've been there, me in Iraq, Dad in Vietnam."

"Don't forget Grandpa in Korea. That's four straight generations of our family in war. I would have loved to have known him." There was a moment of silence between them, each with his own thoughts of their family's saga.

Dave finally broke their musings. "Yeah, Grandpa's the one who didn't make it home, at least in recent history. Dad promised himself he would make it back from Vietnam so his mom wouldn't have to lose anyone else. Dad was sure he would lose a limb, but he was determined to make it home. That's why he practiced lighting his Zippo with both hands – just in case. Guess Dad got luckier than he expected."

The brothers then discuss their dad's story about his buddy Porter. He was the one who did not make the jump in Vietnam.

Their dad and Porter were GIs sitting under a tree in rain ponchos during a monsoon. They were on the bank of the Han River, smoking and talking. They commiserated about being stuck with fruit cocktail instead of peaches, and joked about how Claude had managed to get more than his share of cigarettes. Thankfully for Porter, Claude was a generous man with a ready way to re-up. He was a radio operator, and all he had to do was to say that he was having equipment problems to hitch a chopper ride to the rear.

Claude told his sons he heard a whistling sound, and even though he called out a warning,

Porter didn't make it. The next thing Claude knew, he was coming up in the water and trying to find his buddy. He was nowhere. Claude said he slapped the water repeatedly before he looked up and saw that the entire area where they had been sitting was gone. He frantically searched the water, but there was nothing. Every time he told that story, their father would call out "Porter, Porter, Porter. Fuck!"

"Dave, did he ever tell you if he found Porter's tags?"

"Yeah, he searched all night and found them in the muck of the Han. Dad said that when he pulled the chain out, the tags sparkled in the moonlight. You know our dad is one tough SOB. I still laugh when Dad strikes that Zippo with alternating hands, sometimes with the left and sometimes the right. I realized he was only striking it with his right hand a few months after you left. I didn't say anything because I knew it was for luck. You know, other than your death he most feared you would lose a limb like his buddy Paul did."

"Thank God we all three made it home alive. Pure damn luck, if you ask me. We all saw friends go to their graves and we see them die again and again in our nightmares – at least I do."

"We all do, Josh. War has a hell of a price. There are the guys who never come back, the ones who are severely injured, and lots of ones like Dad and me. We were fucked up for a while and we don't want you to make the same mistakes. When we were kids, I couldn't understand what was wrong with Dad, then when I got back, I understood what he had gone through. Still, I couldn't even talk to him about it when I came home. He tried – it was my fault. Different wars, same battles! We've gotten a lot closer because we finally found something in common – worrying about you."

The day is turning into dusk and the ocean breeze is getting cooler. A beautiful sky is filled with red, yellow, and orange for the coming sunset as the car continues up the highway. They silently admire the scenery, spending time together unencumbered by chatter. The radio and whistling wind do their talking for them.

Josh breaks the precious silence. "I'm not going to make those mistakes. I know you're both here for me. Lucy sees it with vets and understands where I've been. I know that's why she sent us on this road trip."

"Just remember that!"

"Dave, Martini got a real kick out of you wanting to take my place in the war zone. When

I told him how you had it all figured out, he laughed 'til he cried! After that, he would tease me with, 'So, are you Josh or Dave, man? I really need to know who I'm talking to.' Martini could be a real clown sometimes. I can still see him with his hands cupped to his face at the tent door, laughing and yelling. 'This is Dave, man! Let me in!' I would call back. 'Dave's not here, man!' He would keep on. 'This is Dave, man! C'mon, let me in!'

The brothers are laughing hysterically over Martini's antics. "So he would stand at the tent door screaming for what seemed like forever! We would act out that legendary comedy skit several times a week. I must admit, I egged him on – it was relief from the boredom. And it reminded me of you. Man, I missed you! By the way, he thought I was crazy for not taking you up on your offer."

"Well, little brother, I'm glad I could provide some chuckles in the zone. Remember those things – they'll be priceless. Those memories of your buddies are the ones you want to keep. I really was ready to go in your place, even considered knocking you in the head and doing it!" Josh seems to zone out for a minute. Dave glances at him, wondering what is going on in his head, even though he thinks he knows. Then Josh turns to Dave.

"I was watching on a computer in the camp as the communications Humvee was trying to take aim for a strike. The convoy was under fire, and the Humvee with Martini and Sims in it took a direct hit. Dave, that was the first night of patrol after I got my short-timer's stick. Same night, the comm Humvee was hit. They both died. I should've been in the vehicle, I should've been killed, not Sims! Maybe I'd have seen it coming and gotten one of my lucky strikes off. I could have saved Martini! Sims should not even have been in that seat, but they sent her to fill the void when they were running out of replacements. Sims was one of the best I'd seen, not FAC, but a well-trained loan from the British Army."

Dave pulls the car over to the side of the road and turns to Josh. "Death comes when it comes. Don't even go there! If you were meant to be in the vehicle, you would've been. Dad was sitting on a log right next to Porter on the Han River – Porter died and Dad lived. That's war! I know you told me Martini wasn't married when we talked, but did Sims have a wife and kids?"

"Dave, Anne Sims had a husband and two boys. There were a lot of women soldiers in Afghanistan. Some had better instincts than me. Sims was really good; it just wasn't her lucky day. I still wonder if I'd been at the controls would things have turned out different."

"I'm sorry, I just assumed Sims was a man. You're right, I see more and more women in fatigues. You said she was one of the best. If you'd been there you'd have been killed. Pure and simple!"

"I know – it's just sometimes, I think maybe…"

"Nope!"

"Yeah, I know, but I just wish they'd made it. Martini was a great guy."

"I know bro. We've all lost pals in battle, and we all feel survivor's guilt. It had me going for a long while." Dave brightened. "How about we give Lucy a call? Seeing her oughta cheer you up and besides, I'm sure she's waiting to hear how it went at the bakery."

"Sounds great!" Josh starts pressing buttons on the iPad.

Lucy pops up onscreen. "Hi honey!"

"Hey baby. Well, now you've just had me sweep a floor in a bakery! Great cookies though!" Lucy laughs, "I see you met Mrs. Gibson. She's a sweet lady and her chocolate chip cookies are the best."

"How did you know about her?"

"I have driven every mile of this trip! I hoped you would find her. After all, almost everybody in Saltwater Creek is young."

"You had this whole meeting arranged in advance? That's pretty sneaky, young lady!"

"The odds were in her favor. Besides, she's always at the bakery. Did Dave park close to it, like I told him to?"

"Yeah, he parked pretty close. You're right about how young everyone is there. I wasn't holding out much hope for finding an old lady at first, but I was determined to complete the mission. I guess it's that military training. Anyway, Mrs. Gibson is a nice lady. I feel badly for her, losing her daughter."

"I know. I'm so sorry that she lost Katie. I knew she needed a soldier to come home from war. After all, Katie died in Iraq and Ashley is headed to Afghanistan in a few days. I decided to loan you to her, so she could have the homecoming she can't have with her daughter. I knew you could help her cope a little more, and give Mrs. Gibson a few words to say to Ashley that might help bring her home. It was a reminder for both of them. There are the lucky ones who make it home okay. Mrs. Gibson is so worried about Ashley."

"Lucy, I met Ashley. She leaves tomorrow, poor kid. We had a talk. Hope she makes it back. I told Mrs. Gibson I'd come to see her, and I think we should do just that. She can use some company while Ashley is gone; someone who knows what it's like to be over there, and someone who knows what it's like to be waiting. You'll go with me, won't you? After all, I figure it can't be too far from where we live, right?"

"Of course we'll go. As for how close it is to home – nice try! You'll have to figure that out for yourself."

Josh knows she won't give in, but he enjoys the game and so does she. "Lucy, you are something else. How'd I get so lucky, and why are you torturing me so? Can't I at least get a hint where we live?"

"Shush! You live in California, and now you need some rest. Dave will check you guys into a hotel for the night. And keep the room service bill under a couple hundred! Love you. Good night!"

"Good night, Luce."

Lucy is determined to be a part of it, but not to play too big a role in Josh's trip. To her, the question is not who Josh loves the most. It is which person he needs today. She is happy to wait for him to return to her after a little chilling with his brother. "Sweet dreams, baby!" Lucy ends the call.

"Well Dave, I guess we aren't driving straight through to wherever I live tonight. Lucy's right, I'm getting tired. How about you?"

"Yeah, I could use a good night's sleep and some food." Dave pulls the car onto the highway, and they continue heading north.

"How about a clue where I live? Never mind, it doesn't matter as long as Lucy's there at the end of the road. I'll be good." Dave is just shaking his head and grinning. "Might as well stop asking, I'm not telling you shit!"

"I know, just checking.

"Always the optimist, bro!"

Dave pulls off the highway and into the parking lot of a small beachside hotel. It looks like it was built in the 1950's. The place seems new despite its obvious age.

It is late in day when Josh and Dave enter the front door of the hotel and check in. The desk clerk is a woman in her mid-twenties. "Hi, we have a reservation for one night."

"Welcome to Seaside Motel. I'm Carla. What is the last name please?"

"Smith – Dave Smith."

Laughing, Carla says, "Really? Your name really is Smith?" Both Dave and Josh nod and chuckle. "Okay, Mr. Smith, please sign here, and I need a driver's license. I have two keys for you. Also, we have a restaurant and bar open until one AM."

Dave passes his license to her and gets the room keys. "We get that a lot. See, I told you – it really is Smith; we're brothers. Thanks. Come on Josh, let's crash for a while and then grab something to eat in the restaurant, if you want."

The men enter the room, choose their beds, and almost immediately, both fall asleep. It has been an eventful day for both. Well after dark, sirens wail outside the hotel room as two fire trucks speed by with their lights flashing. Josh screams, "Incoming, get down!" as he yanks his brother to the floor between the beds. Dave hits his head on the nightstand and lands on the floor with a thud. Josh is on top of him.

"No, Josh! It's okay! You're home – we're in the hotel. You can get off me now."

In a split second, Josh realizes where they are and sits up, soaked in sweat. Both of them are stunned and sitting with their backs against the beds.

"Shit man, I'm sorry! I really thought bombs were coming in."

Dave gently touches the back of his head. "Yeah I thought so too for a moment. We're all right, except for the bruise on my head. I guess it's just one more war-related head trauma for me." He grins.

Josh still seems alarmed. "Are you okay? I'm soaked with sweat. At least I'm breathing, right?"

"Yeah, we're both fine, but that's a hell of a way to wake up from a nap!" They start laughing and help each other up.

Dave looks at his brother, still shaking as he sits rocking on the bed. "So, how about that drink? I think we could use it."

"Hell yeah, but I need a shower first! I'm drenched!"

After they clean up and calm down, Josh and Dave head to the restaurant, taking a table in back. "Damn, I could use a drink even more than chow, and I'm super hungry! Dave, I'm beginning to understand how much I needed this time."

"Yeah, I hear ya. The menu looks good. Now about that drink..."

Carla arrives at the table, "Hello, gentlemen, how are you doing, Mr. and Mr. Smith?"

Josh looks up at the waitress, "Wow! They must have you working day and night."

Dave chimes in, "I hope you're paid well!"

"Well, not exactly. My family owns this place, so I kinda have no choice! What will you have?" Josh calls out, "The biggest rib eye you got: medium-rare, baked potato, and a Jack and Coke. Not in that order!"

"Same, please."

"Okay great, I'll get the drinks and your food will be out soon."

Dave looks around the restaurant. "This is a nice place, quiet. Lucy did good."

"So you haven't been here before?"

"Nope – it's all your wife."

"So where are we going from here? Should I guess? Man, I really needed that nap." The drinks arrive.

"Well, I didn't need a clunk on the head!" Dave chuckles. "You'll call Lucy tomorrow to find what's next. I'm sure she'll enjoy telling you. And I'm not gonna cross her, so don't even try. How are you feeling?"

"Good, I'm doing okay, just hungry. It's great to be home, yet so strange."

Dave nods, "It was surreal for a while when I first got back from Iraq, especially when I first woke up, and every time I entered or left a room. But it gets better, bro. I'm sure you're ready for a steak. I'd have taken you out for one for lunch. But Lucy planned everything, and I'm following the plan to the letter."

"She was right. I told her on Skype the things I missed most while I was in Afghanistan. You know, stuff like burgers and surfing." Josh looks at his watch then looks to Dave, "Hard to believe seventy-one hours ago, I was halfway around the world at war in the damn mountains of Afghanistan."

"It'll take time for the shock of being home to wear off. It's pretty weird for a while."

"I know there's no magic bullet, Dave – forgive the pun – but I feel like this is helping me chill. Lucy was right. I love her more than anything, but it was you I needed today."

When Lucy planned the map, she decided that the best thing would be for Josh to spend it with someone who had been to war. They would share common ground. He could talk about his experiences and feelings with someone who understood better than she could ever hope to. Josh's words showed he clearly agreed.

Dave gave his brother a smile. "Good. We wanted you to have a chance to relax and unwind without any pressures or expectations. When I heard her plan, I knew it was a good thing. Hey, here are those hunks of beef!"

Carla places the food on the table. "Enjoy guys. If you need anything, just wave."

Both brothers reply together, "Thanks."

The conversation continues. "You know, we suggested Dad come too. Then in his deep voiced Dad impression, Dave tells Josh, 'This is a young man's road trip. I'd just be in the way. You boys have some fun without the old man around. There'll be plenty of time for Josh and me to catch up once he gets here. He needs the time alone with you. I'll make myself useful around here, helping Lucy.' He just adores her! Everyone does."

Carla approaches the table again, "Here's some steak sauce. Let me know if you want anything. Actually, I really like working here, and my folks are great to me. This is just another day in paradise for me. We don't get real busy this time of year, so I have some time to relax. I'll be leaving for a real desert paradise in a month."

Josh asks, "Oh, vacation?"

"Nope, I'm being deployed in a month to Afghanistan, like I said a desert paradise."

"Hey, I've been to paradise. It's not all desert there; there's lots of rocks and mountains, too. I just got back this morning and I'm on my way home. I'm Josh, by the way, and this is my brother Dave. Oh, yeah, you know him; you saw his license."

"Wow! Congrats on being back! In some ways, it's going to be a vacation compared to this little town. I've been here all my life. I'm going to be in the bomb disposal unit, I hear. At least that's what I've been told. I want to be a mechanical engineer, so that's where they want to put me."

Dave's eyes light up when he hears bomb disposal unit, "Hey, that's real important. It's hard, though."

Carla tilts her head slightly looking a little confused. "Why's that, other than not getting blown up?"

Josh begins to tell her, "Carla, if that turns out to be your assignment, its real high risk. It's not like being an engineer. You'll be boots on the ground in a place where IED's are all over. Take that serious. I mean it's extremely high risk.

Sometimes you're on the ground without the minesweeper. Get to know the computer geeks in the comm tents. If you want, I'll give you my information. The comm guys can get you a call out, and I'll be happy to talk whenever you can."

"That'd be great, here," as she hands him a pen. "Use a napkin. I guess the recruiter made bomb disposal sound better than it really is."

As Josh writes his number on the napkin, Dave says in a cold voice, "No shit! They always do!"

Josh tells Carla, "If you need advice or just wanna vent, give me a shout whenever, day or night."

"Thanks, I will. Anything else you can tell me?"

"Remember to look both ways and then back again. Traps are everywhere, IED's and other stuff. Also, since you'll be working with a disposal unit, be careful of anyone, any age that approaches you. Civilians stand in the distance all the time. But if they approach, be careful. They strap bombs on kids. If they don't have a friendly military uniform, be super cautious. Even if they do, you can't be sure unless you know the soldier. Be safe. This is no vacation! You'll wish you were home ten minutes after you land in the war zone. Things have lightened a little since Bin Laden was taken out, but it's still rough over there with lots of action."

"Thanks, Josh. I knew it wasn't paradise; that's just my way of coping with what's coming. Sounds like I'll regret telling them I was interested in an engineering degree. Enjoy your dinner; the next drink is on me. Welcome home again."

Dave tells Carla, "Good luck!"

Josh smiles, "Thanks Carla. It's good to be back home, and good luck to you."

"Thanks for the advice. I'll remember.

The guys are eating while they talk. What few people were in the small restaurant have left. "Josh, No matter how you try to prepare someone for war, there's no way."

"I know, but what you said to me helped. At least I wasn't blind-sided. And when I arrived, I was on high alert, and I stayed that way the whole time I was there."

"It's good to hear that I was able to help some."

"Dave, when I arrived at Gangikhel, I came into camp out of a chopper. They had lost two comm soldiers in a week. I remember you saying to hit the ground low with my gun ready. I did, and thought about you when I realized no one was shooting. You called it a good day if no one was firing at me when I landed."

"Every day when you aren't in the crosshairs is a good day!"

"Hell, yeah! I don't think I'll ever forget seeing the first dead body in Afghanistan. It's not like the pictures they show you. The day I arrived, there were two new comm operators in the chopper with me. Then after I landed, they were bringing bodies back in trucks, including their last FAC guy. We were replacements for the dead. Later, there weren't any more FACs available. That's how Sims came to camp, pure and simple."

"Josh, you'll always remember that first day, and the first body. I do. For a while, a smell or a sound would trigger memories of the bad days for me. Like a ripe dumpster. I'd flash back to the first really bad body I saw. Over time, it happens less. Now, I only do that once in a great while."

"One smell I won't forget is opium. I don't expect to see a lot of that here."

"This is where it gets tricky, Josh. There's opium cologne. If you're not familiar with it, it could trigger a flashback because you still have a strong memory of drug's scent. Tell Lucy to pick up some of that cologne and try to desensitize you to it."

"Never thought of that. The opium odor was good, and nothing really bad happened around me when I smelled it."

Dave continues in a serious tone, "That's what I mean about tricky. Something that you remember as good can suddenly trigger a bad memory. A smell can take you back there, and then all hell can break loose in your head. We definitely need to desensitize you to a few perfumes and other smells, just as a precaution."

"I'll try to come up with a list of things I smelled for the first time while I was there. I'll tell Lucy, and in case I forget, you remind me. I wonder if fruit cocktail would do it? Anything you guys haven't thought of?"

"Damn, I hope not! We're just doing the best we can. I did talk a lot about this with Dad and Lucy. Like you said, we don't have a magic bullet to fix everything."

"Well, you're doing a pretty damn good job at predicting the obstacles ahead of me!"

"I had to jump a bunch of the same hurdles, and more than a couple tripped me up. We're just trying to make it a little better for you than it was for us. I think you're going to be fine. It took years for me to be as calm as you are now. When I came back from Iraq and heard all the people around me at Dover... I know they meant well – but I froze, couldn't move. It was just too much all at once."

"Good to hear you think I'm doing okay! Are you ready to get some shut-eye? Let's suck down that free drink and go." Josh rubs his hands over his head feeling the day catch up to him, "I guess I'm still on Afghan time. I'm bushed!"

"Sounds like a good time to hit the hay, then." They finish dinner and head to the room. Both brothers just collapse onto the beds.

The bond of soldiers is like few other human bonds. The brothers' shared experiences and their understanding of the realities of war were precisely what Lucy had in mind to help Josh. The unselfish act of letting Dave bring him home was to be, in the end, best for her.

Josh tells Dave, "'Night, Cheech."

"Night, Chong." Light laughter fills the room, and then silence takes over.

Josh wakes up first in the morning, "Rise and shine, bro! It's time to call Lucy! Come on!"

Half awake and still wiping the sleep out of his eyes, Dave tries to respond. "Good morning."

Josh is wide awake and full of energy, "I called for coffee and I'm setting up the iPads so we can check in."

"Sure. Just ten more minutes."

"Sorry, I'm still doing the military thing. I wake up hard and fast, especially after some real sleep."

"No shit – I found that out during what I thought would be a peaceful nap! I'm not in the military now, bucko! I need time to pry my eyes open." Josh is setting up the iPads on the dresser, as the coffee arrives and Dave rolls out of bed. "How'd you sleep, Josh?"

"Out completely. Not a thought, once I hit the bed."

Dave is pulling on his jeans, "Perfect! Let me get my clothes on before you Skype."

"Hurry up, slowpoke! I'm dialing."

"Damn Josh, let me get a shirt on!"

Just then, Lucy pops up onscreen. "Good morning baby, did you rest well?"

"Yes, but there was a little incident while we took a nap before dinner. Seems that fire trucks bother me. I'll tell you about it later. We had dinner in the motel restaurant and I slept like a baby last night.

"Are you okay?" Lucy's face shows concern.

"I'm fine, but Dave has a knot on his head."

"What happened? What did you do to him?"

"I was protecting him from a bomb – I pulled him off the bed and onto the floor."

"Is he all right?"

Dave chimes in, "Morning Lucy. I'm fine, it's just a little tender, but I forgot how much he snores. Lucky you!" Josh throws a pillow across the room, hitting Dave in the chest.

"I didn't hear me snoring at all! I had a huge rib eye for dinner, and enjoyed every bite. I went out to the car to get the iPads this morning, and I'm still amazed that the boards fit in there. She looks so beautiful, just like you!"

"Well, we didn't change the size of the trunk when we redid her, so the boards should fit just like they always did. You both look like you need showers. You're headed to Santa Barbara first to parasail or find a spot for lunch. Do whatever sounds good. See you soon. Enjoy yourselves. Love you!" Lucy is still being very careful not to put pressure on Josh and just be a small part of the trip.

"Notice how your wife hangs up fast right after she tells you what's next, leaving me to take the shit for it!"

"I'm not giving you any shit. I'm having a hell of a good time, and parasailing sounds fun to me!"

"I know; I'm just busting on Lucy!" They gather themselves and head up the winding road again looking for the perfect place to stop and soak in some more sun in Santa Barbara. Finally, Dave pulls the car to a stop.

"Remember when Mom and Dad would bring us here? You were pretty young then."

"Yeah, we're California kids. I brought Luce here, since we didn't have time for a real honeymoon. She grew up in Venice Beach and just loves Santa Barbara, too."

"The day you met her was the luckiest day of your life, next to the one when you got out of Afghanistan alive. She's a keeper!

"Did you know a bunch of vets she treats at the VA have been working alongside Dad at your new house? JD, an Iraqi vet, is a genius with electricity. He got started with it 'cause he had to rewire the damn showers in Iraq after the contractors screwed 'em up. He and other vets put a lot of sweat into your place. Mom, Linda, and Lucy did the cooking for the whole crew.

"JD and Dad get along great. They're both Harley guys, and they even started riding together when they weren't rehabbing the house. They're hanging out together a lot, now that most of the work is done.

"I think the vets have found a new hobby after working on your new digs. They're helping fix up each others' houses, now that Dad doesn't need them for yours. But every one of 'em said they'll come running if you need some help with anything else.

"Did you know Lucy picked up every overtime shift she could at the hospital all the time you were deployed? She said that she was glad to do it to help soldiers at the VA."

Josh appears concerned as he replies to Dave. "I'm sure the vets like her – who doesn't? I'm a little nervous, though – I knew she was working a lot, but I didn't realize she was taking every shift. We shouldn't have needed money that bad. What the hell did she buy?"

"Josh, she didn't do it for the money. She said that besides helping people, it kept her mind busy so she wouldn't be worrying about you all the time. She wanted to get you guys ahead of the game. That way, you could spend some time together when you got back without being strapped for cash. We all offered to float a loan, but she insisted on doing it herself. Her leave started today; she worked first shift yesterday, and then she went home to work on your place."

"How bad is this house? It sounds like it took an awful lot of work."

"It's no palace, but a lot of labor by a bunch of old GIs has made it livable, and you can take it from there."

"Well, if it's habitable, that's good enough for now, 'cause I want us to have the honeymoon we didn't get before I left. You're right – I'm a lucky man. I've got great parents, some new friends from the VA, a reasonably okay brother, and Lucy, the love of my life!"

"Now that you're home, relax and enjoy your new wife. Don't be afraid to talk to her about the war. You probably should skip the gory details. Lucy is strong and she's been following everything going on over there. But if it gets too much, you call me day or night! I made lots of mistakes when I got back, and it nearly cost my marriage. I held everything in and couldn't come to terms what I've seen. It took a psychiatrist to sort it out, 'cause I waited too long to ask for help. You know, I got lost in the bottle for a while. Don't do that. Keep it a down to couple of drinks, just like you used to."

"I hear you, and I'll do it. One thing is causing me a lot of stress right now, and I'm sure you can help me with it."

"What's that? You know I'll help if I can."

Josh starts laughing. "You could tell me… you're really not going to tell me where I live?"

"No way, but she did good! Now let's parasail, maybe walk on the beach, and then we'll call Lucy." They head out on parasails over the water and return to the beach excited and hungry.

"Wow that was awesome! I'd forgotten just how much good stuff I've been missing out on."

"The winds are amazing today. Josh, I haven't sailed since you left. I know this trip is for you, but no reason I can't enjoy it, too. I needed that!"

"Happy to share! The feeling of the wind on me – that's something you just don't get in Afghanistan! There, if a breeze blows, it's full of grit."

They sit on the beach looking at each other. Each one sees themselves as young boys and as they are now. Every story is told with fond memories of their lives as brothers and the commonality of soldiers. After a while, they become quiet, lost in their own memories. Josh broke the comfortable silence. "Remember when Dad taught us to surf here?"

"Yeah, the old man can still ride a curl."

They get up and head to the car, trying to shake off the sand.

"Dave it looks like like your old war wound isn't bothering you much now. Your knee seems fine."

"It's doing okay. When I was a sniper, all that kneeling in firing positions really screwed with it, but I'm doing good. Lucy made me do physical therapy again while you were gone. I whined but followed orders. I have to admit, the therapy sucked, but I think it did help some."

"Well, it looked like it worked while you were out there. Nice landing."

"You know, I messed it up when I was in Al Khafji. I was covered in camouflage and setting up my rifle in some broken building trying to guard a supply convoy coming through the town. I saw the insurgents setting up a grenade launch site and picked them off one by one like birds on a wire and the convoy was able to roll safely through. The entire time my knee was on the sharp edge of the building. Tore it up! It still bothers me some."

Dave reaches to rub his knee by habit. "It gets stiff, but at least I can do most everything, thanks to Lucy. It was getting pretty bad again for a while. Still, if that's my only war wound, I shouldn't complain. After all, we all made the decision to go. Well, except Dad.

"How come?"

"Well, Dad got drafted, but he could've gone to Canada. Plenty of guys did. Instead, he went to 'Nam. So I suppose he made the choice to fight, as well."

Dave thinks it is time for Josh to be desensitized a bit more. "I have a few firecrackers. Let's set them off. I just wanted you to hear the sound again. It may help when you hear one unexpectedly."

"Makes sense – besides, it's fun." The brothers set off the firecrackers near the water's edge. "Got any more?"

"Nope, that's all I brought. Just remember, something like this or the sound of a backfire may cause you to duck and cover, no matter where you are. Don't be embarrassed or mad at yourself. Just get up and say, 'that move kept me alive.' If you're with other people, tell 'em that. If you're alone, say it to yourself. Never feel bad about that reaction, no matter where you are!"

"Got it! Dave, I kind of wish Dad had come with you. This has been great, but now I'm missing him too. Can you imagine all three warriors together?"

"Well, if you want to make the old man's day, I know he's hoping for a call. He told me he'd meet us if you really wanted him to, but he didn't want to intrude on our time together."

"Let's do it! How about The 17th Parallel? I know it's not on Lucy's map, but..."

"You still don't get her map. It's just a guide, with a few mandatory stops. It's not orders chiseled into stone. We're on a ride!"

"I want to see Dad! Come on!"

"Okay, but we're not in a war zone, dropping spent shell casings as we go. We don't leave firecracker bits lying around, strewn all over the sand. You're back in the US of A!" They pick up the bits of firecracker casings and head to the car where Josh gets out his iPad.

"Call Lucy and let me talk to her this time, Josh."

Josh calls Lucy.

"Hello guys. What's up?"

"Lucy, is Dad there?"

"Sure, let me get him off the ladder." Claude gets on camera. "Hey boys. Having fun?"

"Dad, 17th Parallel, thirty minutes!"

"Wahoo! Roger that, Dave!" He races from the house.

Lucy is back on camera. "Well, Dad is gone in a flash! You two just made his day! He's been hoping for a call."

"Hey baby, that's Dad's favorite restaurant!"

"Yeah, and it's got a bar, too! Love you, hon. Have fun. But you guys behave, now! I have three soldiers on the loose; there's no telling what you'll get into."

The 17th Parallel is an old place with good food and great drinks. Most of the customers are ex-military. Josh and Dave walk into the restaurant and join Claude, who is already sitting at a table. He gets up and hugs his son so tightly that Josh has to catch his breath. All three generations sitting together almost look like a Norman Rockwell painting.

"Damn, it's good to see you, son! Skype was great while you were gone, but that machine is not the same as seeing you in person, boy!"

"Dad, it's good to see you, too! I saw Jim behind the counter when we came in. I'm surprised the restaurant is so empty, though. I've never seen it like this. Slow day, I guess. It's just us in here. Damn, this is great – all three of us! How's Mom?"

"Your mom is fine. She's with Lucy. She loves that girl like the daughter we never had. Listen Josh, this place is empty because I called from the car. All of the folks that were in here are in the back lot. Jim put them there so they wouldn't all mob you at once. We wanted to make sure it's okay for them to say hi. There are about 15 out there. You know most all of them. They promise to make it short. Are you okay with that?"

Josh's laugh fills the place. "I knew something was up. It has never been this slow in here. Damn right I'm okay with it! Let those poor folks in! I was beginning to think this place was going out of business!"

Claude yells out, "Jim! It's okay let 'em in." Jim heads to the back door of the restaurant. Claude tells the boys, "This place will last as long as soldiers still go into battle and come home from war! Jim says he'd be happy to change the name if they'd just stop making us fight." A group of people from all three wars comes in the back door. They are applauding. There are men and a few women. They are mostly vets, but some are still active duty.

One vet, Mike, starts to talk. "Josh, welcome home from all of us! In the parking lot, I got elected to make a little speech. I'll be short."

Claude starts laughing. "Mike, you never made anything short in your life!"

"I'm trying. If you'd quit interrupting, Claude, I'd almost be done already! Josh, we're all so damn glad you're back home safe. I'll keep this short, so you guys can enjoy your time together and we can get back to our food."

Josh motions to the food jokingly. "It's cold now, guys!"

"I hear ya, Josh, but we don't care about the food. We're just damn glad to have you home. We've all been where you are; the first few days back from war. And most of us knew about Lucy's map. The rest found out in the parking lot. What a gal you have! You know she comes in with Dad and Dave. We love her! She has inspired a bunch of us to take a decompression trip, even though some of us have been home for years. We all agreed – no one would leave to follow their map until you made it home. Dan is taking his son, Mark is taking his wife, Karen is taking her bother, Phil is going with a buddy from Vietnam, and so on! All thanks to Lucy's idea."

Mike continues, "If guys gotta go to battle, seeing three generations in the same family back alive from war and sitting at a table together is all any of us could wish for. You, Dave, and Claude have given so much, and we salute you! Thank you again, and welcome home, soldier! Now, enjoy! If you don't mind, some of us may stop by your table on the way out." The patrons start to go back to their tables.

"Wow! Thanks, everybody! You've all made coming home even better, if that was possible! Thanks again and of course if anyone wants to stop by the table, feel free! Hey, Jim can they get a reheat on the food and round of drinks on me? Not Dave though, he's driving me. I don't have a clue where I live. Anyone gonna tell me?"

All of the vets respond as one. "Hell, no!" Then Claude tells Josh, "Not a chance. No way I'm getting on Lucy's bad side; she'd have my ass for sure! I think a little mystery is a good thing! I ain't sayin' shit, but I know you'll like it."

Jim calls out from behind the counter, "Are you kidding? Lucy has us all trained! You got it on the drinks, Josh! But they're on the house, and Josh, you can have as many as you want on me. Too bad for Dave!" The group claps at the free drinks.

Dave tells Jim, "I didn't make it back from war and through LA traffic with Josh, just to die in a car accident! Still, I can have one, so I can drink a toast."

"Oh, all right, I guess you oughta be able to raise a glass to your brother."

"I'm glad you see my point Jim. Make it a great big...Pepsi. Gotcha!" There is more laughter in the room and the soldiers continue their own conversations.

"Dad, as soon as Josh said he was sorry you didn't come along, we had to make the call." "Thanks, Dave. This is great! It sure is!"

"I'm surprised you didn't come with Dave to pick me up. We've had fun!"

Claude says with his deep laugh, "Well I didn't want to interfere with your road trip – didn't want the old man slowing down the young'uns." Then in a more serious voice, "Josh how you doing, really?"

"Dad, I'm good. Coming home this way, with Lucy's map and Dave easing me back into society has been the best thing for me. I can feel the difference from when the plane landed. "

"So you were wound like a twelve day clock when you got off the plane, son?"

"Hell, you know it! I'm still winding down now. Cruising around with him is perfect."

"Good, good! Dave, so how's he really doing?"

"Dad, Josh is coping great, and he made us a promise. He won't get mad at us if we see him having trouble and try to help him."

"So, not going to be an asshole like your brother and I were when we came back? Good! Your mother and Lucy will be very happy to hear that!"

"Dad, I'm gonna try to learn from my elders' mistakes. I'm gonna work hard at chilling. I think I'm doing a fine-ass job of it, so far! I know I have you guys and our family to get me through the tough times. I'm feeling more comfortable in my own skin now. Thanks."

Claude raises his drink to cheer his sons, "A toast to my boys! Home alive!"

Just after the glasses clink, Dave tells Claude, "Um, Dad... Martini died."

"Shit, Josh! I'm sorry, son. I put my foot in my mouth again. I know he was your buddy. Damn! What happened? Do you even want to talk about it?"

"Yeah, it's all right. It was a direct hit on a Humvee. He was with another friend of mine, Sims. They were attacked the day after I got my short-timer's stick. Sims was my replacement. They were both great soldiers."

"Damn son, that's hard. I know I had a real rough time when Porter died. If he had just jumped into the fucking river! Well, no point in the wouldas and shouldas. I'm very sorry. You know, I still remember the day the soldiers came to the house to tell us your grandpa died in Taejon, Korea. It was 1950. Two uniformed Marines came to the front door to deliver a Killed in Action notification. I was just a young boy. We saw them from inside the house through a screened door. I can still hear my mother screaming. I cried because she cried. Don't think I really understood it then. You would've like your grandpa."

With a smile, Josh tells his dad, "I'm sure I would have. I always wondered what he was like; wish I'd had a chance to know him. I'm sorry he didn't make it – for your sake and grandma's. I know it had to be hard on you, growing up without a dad."

"I barely knew him. But I remember playing catch, riding on his shoulders, and that I loved him. The advantage of him dying when I was young is that I didn't know any different; it was always just your grandmother and me. It was awfully hard on her. She never did get over losing him. I'm so glad those short-timer's sticks were good luck for both of you."

Dave looks up at his dad, "Yeah, I guess they were, Dad. You know, after I got my stick, there was a raid on our camp in Iraq. I got out, but my buddy Lerner didn't. He was asleep on the cot right next to me. War doesn't make sense."

"I'm sorry, Dave. I didn't know."

"Yeah, I'm sorry too, bro. I didn't know that either. Dad, Sims, the soldier who was with Martini, she had plenty of experience. It was just the luck of the draw, I guess, an unlucky day for both of 'em."

"Boys, it's never easy to lose a friend."

"Sims was a damn good soldier; as good as any man. She was spot on! However, she was not even supposed be to be sent in there, but when there is a shortage of trained controllers, they send who they can find. She was a loan from the British. I feel for her family."

Dave looks to Josh in sympathy. "We had a few women in the combat area in Iraq who died, but I heard the numbers were increasing in Afghanistan."

"Yeah, the Vietnamese had women fighters, but we didn't in 'Nam. I think we could've ended the war earlier if women had been there. I mean damn, you don't want to piss them off. They think faster than us most of the time. I know your mom does! We used to say, send some pissed off mothers to war, and they'll end 'em all. I think it's true, but it's still hard for me to imagine women in battle next to me."

Dave lifts his glass in toast, "A toast to all heroes! The real ones who didn't make it back! You fought a good fight and we'll never forget you."

All the vets in the restaurant raise their glasses, "Here! Here!"

Josh puts his drink down and smiles at his father, "Dad, so you've taken a shine to Lucy."

"Where did you find that girl? She's a real gem, like Linda and your mom! Just can't figure out what she sees in you."

Josh has a big smile at his father's approval of Lucy, "Let's face it, we all got lucky. I mean, hell, they put up with us. They may be crazy, but thank God they love us enough to endure our weirdness!"

Dave tells his brother, "Josh, if you mess up, we get to keep Lucy and get rid of your sorry ass! So don't screw up! I'd hate to make that choice, 'cause I've kinda got used to having a little brother!"

Claude quickly joins in, "I second that. I don't want to disown you, but losing Lucy? I don't know… you might just lose that fight!"

Claude turns serious again. "Josh, what was Afghanistan like? I mean, I know it isn't like the jungle and swampland I was in. I hear it was desert as far as you can see."

"It was like that Dad, but they have a lot of mountains, and that's where the enemy hid. We had to struggle to find them, but we did. It was rough, you know, the first few times you see death. Then you become almost numb to it, like a dream you can't wake up from. There were bodies all over."

"Yeah, same as the jungle or Iraq, I imagine. I had the same damn nightmare, but the faces blended until I couldn't remember anything about my life before the war. I saw death everywhere. It really screws with your head. The shittiest part was when I got home to your mother. I was a jerk. I'm so thankful she stayed and helped me through it. Like I said, I think women are stronger than us in many ways. I'd never admit it to 'em, and don't you dare tell 'em I said that!"

A look of agreement washes over Dave's face. "That's true for me, too. I couldn't have survived alone. When I first got to Iraq, I was petrified at all the death around me, and no way out but straight through. Then when I returned I had to face it. Those guys are now, gone forever. I felt like no one could ever understand. Trying to cope seemed useless, but finally I did."

Claude gives a look of approval and kindness to Dave. It is obvious to Josh that they have been through much together. His deployment brought them closer, allowed them a way to share their inner thoughts, and gave them a common goal. A simple look can say so much. "Dave, you have a firm grip on things now. I'm proud of you."

"Me too, bro."

Dave looks to Josh, "Forgetting isn't easy Josh and the bottom line is you'll never forget it all. You will learn to adjust and hopefully to keep the good memories of your buddies in your mind but forget most of the bad stuff. Look around at what you have, not what you don't. It helps a lot!"

Claude's eyes light up, "So Josh, do the women there really wear those burka things? Can you imagine me telling your mom she has to do that? She would have killed me herself!"

Josh laughs, "Yeah right, try that on mom and she'd have your ass! Seriously, women are controlled by the tribes. They use fear and treat 'em like animals that can be easily killed and replaced. Some women try to fight back in their own way. Most often, those they end up dead. Do you know if a woman is raped she can be put to death for infidelity? It happens a lot there, and not by foreign soldiers. As if they had a choice about it! I just don't get it."

Claude is shocked. "Women weren't treated like that in Vietnam. They were strong and lots of 'em were pretty. I think they woulda killed the men if anyone tried that!"

Dave almost seems lost as he started to ask, "What is wrong with some people? Why do they do these things?"

"I guess they do it because they can, son. That's sure not a reason."

Josh nods. "Yeah, I agree. You couldn't even see women's' faces. They're not allowed to show any skin; those burkas even cover their eyes. They can see out, but no one can see in. If a married woman gets caught looking at another man, she's beaten in public. Women can't go to school. They are treated like cattle and used as baby factories. It's sick! We had Muslim soldiers in the Marines and they couldn't understand these tribes, either."

Dave seems to be still shocked at this part of war. "I know what you mean. It's sad, though. In Iraq, they're mostly Muslim and just nice people in the hell of war. I didn't see a lot of women, because the crazy zealots tribes were keeping them in burkas. Man, Linda would never go for anyone telling her what to do. I wouldn't want that. I like her being independent. I mentioned once I didn't like a dress, so she wore it more. Oh, hell no, I can't even imagine it! Linda rules our house. I don't mind at all. A happy wife is a happy life!"

Claude clears his throat. "Well I rule our house, you both know that!"

Josh starts laughing. "Okay, Dad. I'll let mom know. I guess she missed the memo."

Dave looks at his watch. "Dad, we need to get back on the road. Thanks for hanging out with us for a while. Tell Linda I'll be home soon and kiss my kids and mom for me."

"Okay boys, I had a blast. You two be safe. I'll see you for the cookout on Sunday at Josh's new place. We planned it for Sunday so you and Lucy have some private time first. Love you both – you are damn good sons."

"Give 'em our love, and I'll be wherever my house is when we finish with Lucy's map. Tell her I love her, and that we are having fun. Tell her I'm okay, but don't tell her that I've figured out we live between Santa Maria and San Luis Obispo!"

"I won't tell her you are guessing. By the way, that was nice going on trying to trick me! She's worked too hard on this map for me to spill the beans about anything. I'll tell her I think you're going to show both of us up adjusting, 'cause I believe it!"

"Thanks Pop, and it's because of you guys and Lucy thinking outside the box! You're right; don't tell her I'm guessing. After all, I still don't know. I'm sure we're within a half hour."

Claude with a grumble tells Josh, "That's a big area out there!" They all say their goodbyes and another round of hugs.

Dave looks to Josh, "Come on Josh, let's get a move on. We can drive some more, then stop for coffee and you can call Lucy later."

"Sounds good! Dad looks great. I'm glad we called him. Now he can go back and tell them I really am here and I'm okay."

"Josh, this map is all about you unwinding from the war. We're on this trip for you. I just wish I had a trip like this planned for me on my way home. You know, someone to chill with who's been there. I know if Linda would have had any idea about what was to come, she woulda done the same thing for me. I'm glad you're doing well and taking advantage of the downtime to chill."

"I sure am! Shit, the D-Map, only Lucy could figure out something this relaxing!"

Then with a laugh, Dave chimes in, "Skype your genius wife."

"You're too much!"

Dave opens the trunk; Josh gets out an iPad and they contact Lucy. She answers in her usual bubbly way. "Having fun with Dad?"

"He just left, and we're getting back on the road. It was great to see him! What's next? We're having a good ol' time!" Josh now has the camera turned so he looks upside down in the car.

Lucy is laughing so hard at how they are acting that she spits her soda out on the camera, "This part is Dave's choice! Take it away – heeeere's Dave!"

"I've got it from here, Lucy. I knew Josh just wanted to see your face!"

Josh smirks. "Yeah – I can't wait to see the rest of you, too."

"I'll be waiting. Love you, hon! Have fun!"

"Bye, baby."

After their coffee stop, Dave turns the car back onto Highway 1. He calls out, "Okay, let's roll."

"I got it… a little tribute to those who fought back against the terrorists over Pennsylvania, flight 93. That's what they said on the plane. Let's roll! Bravo heroes! Nice one!"

Not too far up the road, Josh sees his old middle school. "Look, Lealman Middle School! Cool, a soccer practice!"

"Yeah, I coach part time on weekends, and Abe will be old enough to play next year."

Dave parks the car and they walk to the bleachers, taking a seat to watch the practice, coffee in hand. They talk about the kids while they watch. The bleachers are nearly empty. As the conversation turns to his children, Dave shakes his head. "I can't believe that next year Abe will be trying out for the soccer team. Lilly too!"

"Wow, already? I've missed so much being away. Do you enjoy coaching?"

"Yeah, I do. Josh, it's unreal that Abe and Lilly will be entering middle school next year. I can't wait. They're good kids. Coaching has helped me a lot since I got out of my own head. For a while, it was hard to hear kids screaming and not flash back to Iraq. Now I hear the laughter, not the terror."

Quietly, in almost a whisper, Josh says, "Dave, a young boy carrying a bomb was running toward a convoy in Afghanistan. I watched as the he was shot by one of our guys who picked him off with a scope. After that, I'm surprised, but I feel like I'm doing okay sitting here watching them practice. It's good for me. They're yelling and moving around without any carnage. I don't have to worry that every kid wants to kill me or will end up dead. I still can't wrap my head around the why. Why would they use children like that? It never made sense to me."

"Yeah, I agree, but I'm sure they figure we wouldn't hurt kids. Recruiting 'em so early and using them like that pisses me off! It took a long time, but now I can relax. I still get some flashbacks, but not so many. It gets better every day."

"I hope so. Overall, I think I'm doing pretty well so far. On a heavier note, you're starting to look like our old coach. Really Dave, you're barely in your thirties! Do you even work out?" Josh pokes Dave in the belly with his finger. "Uh-huh! Flabby!"

"Watch it bro! What's the crack about my weight? I can still run circles around you!"

"Maybe, with a break here and there, but I doubt it."

"I think we should get moving, Josh. I just wanted you to hear the sound of kids laughing. Come on; let's get back on the road." Dave takes off running with a head start. "Beat you to the car!"

"Cheater! No fair, you took off first!"

As they approach the parked car, Josh asks for the keys to drive. "Toss me the keys. I'm ready to give her a spin!"

"Lucy said when you were ready to go home, you'd ask for the keys. Are you?"

"I am, but I'm so glad we did this trip! It's helped me wind down. But now, it's time to see Luce."

"Okay. Linda will pick me up here, 'cause you're heading home on your own. Take some time to have that honeymoon get. We're going to barbecue – just the family – on Sunday."

"Sounds great!"

"Josh, you won't forget what happened, but you'll learn to cope. A boy goes to war but a man returns. About that question you asked – Why? Your country called and you answered. That's the only understanding you'll ever find.

"Thanks, Dave. Hearing that makes me feel better."

Now, it's time for you to live on and love Lucy. She's a great gal."

"But I still have one big problem – will somebody tell me where in the hell I live? You gonna finally give it up?"

"Nope; you gotta guess! Just turn on the nav system Lucy had installed in the glove box. It's programmed for home. The key is on the ring."

"Wait! You said you didn't have a key!"

"No, I said Lucy must have locked it."

"Smooth! Later bro. Thanks for everything!"

"Welcome home, Josh! Remember, if you need anything, we're here."

With a smile and a long embrace, the brothers part company. Josh drives away as Linda is pulling into the parking lot. He heads up the Scenic Coast Highway. The Beach Boy's California Girls is blasting from the stereo when the nav system says he's arrived.

Josh sees nothing more than a shack with a large, painted wooden sign out front. The building is in desperate need of repair, but it has a million dollar view of the beach. Josh gets out of the car, surprised at where the GPS has brought him. Lucy is sitting on a small stretch of beach, waiting in one of two chaises. She turns her head for the hundredth time, looking for Josh. She finally sees what she has been waiting for. He's home! There is no hesitation as they rush together for a long-awaited kiss.

"Baby, I missed you! I thought the GPS system was taking me home, but home is wherever you are!"

"You are home! This place is what I bought. It's ours."

Josh is astonished. "This is ours? This beach property? How can we afford it?"

As they walk slowly hand in hand, Lucy tells him the story of the shack. "Well, my father owned it, and I used to come here when I was a kid. I thought he had gotten rid of it years ago. When I mentioned our dream of one day living on the beach, he told me he still had it, and he would sell it to us for practically nothing. We may live in a shack for now, but it's clean on the inside. We'll have plenty of time to do more work on it.

"Are you kidding? It's absolutely perfect! You made our dream come true!"

Lucy points to the wooden sign. "You can take that down now, if you'd like. After all, it's our house – our home."

Josh looks into Lucy's eyes. "I kind of like the sign just where it is. I think it should stay." He grins as he reads it aloud.

"Bait Shop Closed"

Every *Decompression Map* is different.

What is yours?

Wounded Warriors

DECOMPRESSION MAP

FOR

_____

Soldiers' Arrival Date:

_____

Location of Arrival:

_____

Arrival Time:

_____

Person/Persons Meeting Returning Soldier:

(The smaller the number of people the better.
Who does soldier need?)

_____

_____

_____

_____

Items to Pack:

Favorite civilian clothes of soldier:
(Shirts, pants, jacket, socks, shoes, skivvies, toothpaste, brush, comb, razor, shave cream, cash, cell phone, telephone numbers of love ones/friends, debit card, gas card, music for car or headset, camera or video camera) and other items of comfort for the trip that the soldier my enjoy and use at will:

_____

_____

_____

_____

_____

_____

_____

_____

_____

_____

List of items needed such as car rental or airline tickets – locations, maps, addresses and telephone numbers, hotel reservation numbers, etc. (Remember, make this a stress-free trip.)

_____

_____

_____

_____

_____

_____

_____

_____

_____

_____

_____

_____

_____

_____

_____

Wounded Warriors

_____

_____

_____

_____

_____

_____

_____

_____

_____

_____

_____

_____

_____

_____

_____

_____

_____

_____

STOPS

(Make suggestions for fun and interesting things to do while at the stops. All should be related to things to that the soldier loved before he/she left for war.)

Stop One Location & Activities

_____

_____

_____

_____

_____

_____

_____

Stop Two Location & Activities

_____

_____

_____

_____

_____

_____

Stop Three Location & Activities

_____

_____

_____

_____

_____

_____

_____

Stop Four Location & Activities

_____

_____

_____

_____

_____

_____

Stop Five Location & Activities

_____

_____

_____

Matrix Filia & Claudette Walker

_____

_____

_____

_____

Stop Six or More Location & Activities

_____

_____

_____

_____

_____

_____

_____

_____

_____

_____

_____

_____

_____

_____

Wounded Warriors

_____

_____

_____

_____

_____

_____

_____

_____

_____

_____

_____

_____

_____

_____

_____

_____

_____

Matrix Filia & Claudette Walker

JOURNAL OF MEMORIES

MY DECOMPRESSION

NAME: _____

DATE(S):_____

Wounded Warriors

_____

_____

_____

_____

_____

_____

_____

_____

_____

_____

_____

_____

_____

_____

_____

_____

_____

_____

Matrix Filia & Claudette Walker

_____

_____

_____

_____

_____

_____

_____

_____

_____

_____

_____

_____

_____

_____

_____

_____

_____

_____

_____

Wounded Warriors

_____

_____

_____

_____

_____

_____

_____

_____

_____

_____

_____

_____

_____

_____

_____

_____

_____

_____

_____

_____

Matrix Filia & Claudette Walker

_____

_____

_____

_____

_____

_____

_____

_____

_____

_____

_____

_____

_____

_____

_____

_____

_____

_____

_____

Wounded Warriors

Matrix Filia & Claudette Walker

Wounded Warriors

_____

_____

_____

_____

_____

_____

_____

_____

_____

_____

_____

_____

_____

_____

_____

_____

_____

_____

Matrix Filia & Claudette Walker

Wounded Warriors

_____

_____

_____

_____

_____

_____

_____

_____

_____

_____

_____

_____

_____

_____

_____

_____

Matrix Filia & Claudette Walker

_____

_____

_____

_____

_____

_____

_____

_____

_____

_____

_____

_____

_____

_____

_____

_____

_____

_____

_____

Wounded Warriors

_____

_____

_____

_____

_____

_____

_____

_____

_____

_____

_____

_____

_____

_____

_____

_____

_____

_____

Matrix Filia & Claudette Walker

Wounded Warriors

_____

_____

_____

_____

_____

_____

_____

_____

_____

_____

_____

_____

_____

_____

_____

_____

_____

_____

Matrix Filia & Claudette Walker

_____

_____

_____

_____

_____

_____

_____

_____

_____

_____

_____

_____

_____

_____

_____

_____

_____

_____

Wounded Warriors

_____

_____

_____

_____

_____

_____

_____

_____

_____

_____

_____

_____

_____

_____

_____

_____

_____

_____

_____

Matrix Filia & Claudette Walker

_____

_____

_____

_____

_____

_____

_____

_____

_____

_____

_____

_____

_____

_____

_____

_____

Wounded Warriors

Matrix Filia & Claudette Walker

Wounded Warriors

_____

_____

_____

_____

_____

_____

_____

_____

_____

_____

_____

_____

_____

_____

_____

_____

_____

_____

Matrix Filia & Claudette Walker

_____

_____

_____

_____

_____

_____

_____

_____

_____

_____

_____

_____

_____

_____

_____

_____

_____

_____

_____

Wounded Warriors

Matrix Filia & Claudette Walker

_____

_____

_____

_____

_____

_____

_____

_____

_____

_____

_____

_____

_____

_____

_____

_____

_____

_____

Wounded Warriors

_____

_____

_____

_____

_____

_____

_____

_____

_____

_____

_____

_____

_____

_____

_____

_____

_____

_____

Matrix Filia & Claudette Walker

Wounded Warriors

_____

_____

_____

_____

_____

_____

_____

_____

_____

_____

_____

_____

_____

_____

_____

_____

_____

_____

_____

_____

Matrix Filia & Claudette Walker

_____

_____

_____

_____

_____

_____

_____

_____

_____

_____

_____

_____

_____

_____

_____

_____

_____

_____

_____

Wounded Warriors

_____

_____

_____

_____

_____

_____

_____

_____

_____

_____

_____

_____

_____

_____

_____

_____

_____

Matrix Filia & Claudette Walker

Wounded Warriors

_____

_____

_____

_____

_____

_____

_____

_____

_____

_____

_____

_____

_____

_____

_____

_____

_____

Matrix Filia & Claudette Walker

_____

_____

_____

_____

_____

_____

_____

_____

_____

_____

_____

_____

_____

_____

_____

_____

_____

_____

Wounded Warriors

_____

_____

_____

_____

_____

_____

_____

_____

_____

_____

_____

_____

_____

_____

_____

_____

_____

Matrix Filia & Claudette Walker

_____

_____

_____

_____

_____

_____

_____

_____

_____

_____

_____

_____

_____

_____

_____

_____

_____

_____

_____

Wounded Warriors

_____

_____

_____

_____

_____

_____

_____

_____

_____

_____

_____

_____

_____

_____

_____

_____

_____

_____

_____

Matrix Filia & Claudette Walker

_____

_____

_____

_____

_____

_____

_____

_____

_____

_____

_____

_____

_____

_____

_____

_____

_____

Wounded Warriors

_____

_____

_____

_____

_____

_____

_____

_____

_____

_____

_____

_____

_____

_____

_____

_____

_____

_____

Wounded Warriors

Matrix Filia & Claudette Walker

_____

_____

_____

_____

_____

_____

_____

_____

_____

_____

_____

_____

_____

_____

_____

_____

_____

_____

Wounded Warriors

_____

_____

_____

_____

_____

_____

_____

_____

_____

_____

_____

_____

_____

_____

_____

_____

_____

_____

_____

_____

_____

Wounded Warriors

Matrix Filia & Claudette Walker

Wounded Warriors

_____

_____

_____

_____

_____

_____

_____

_____

_____

_____

_____

_____

_____

_____

_____

_____

_____

_____

Matrix Filia & Claudette Walker

_____

_____

_____

_____

_____

_____

_____

_____

_____

_____

_____

_____

_____

_____

_____

_____

_____

_____

Wounded Warriors

Matrix Filia & Claudette Walker

Wounded Warriors

Matrix Filia & Claudette Walker

_____

_____

_____

_____

_____

_____

_____

_____

_____

_____

_____

_____

_____

_____

_____

_____

_____

_____

_____

_____

Wounded Warriors